Reckless Night

&

Hot Secrets

RECKLESS NIGHT

A Dangerous Passion Novella

LISA MARIE RICE

HOT SECRETS

A Dangerous Lover Novella

AVONIMPULSE

Excerpt from *Dangerous Lover* copyright © 2007 by Lisa Marie Rice
Excerpt from *Dangerous Secrets* copyright © 2008 by Lisa Marie Rice
Excerpt from *Dangerous Passion* copyright © 2009 by Lisa Marie Rice

RECKLESS NIGHT EPub Edition December 2011 ISBN: 9780062115218
HOT SECRETS EPub Edition January 2012 ISBN: 9780062115225

Print Edition ISBN: 9780062195500

FIRST EDITION

10 9 8 7 6 5 4 3 2 1

RECKLESS NIGHT

Manuel Rabat opened his present with a heavy heart, knowing it would be absolutely perfect because his absolutely perfect wife, Victoria, was a world-class artist.

Even the fucking wrapping paper was perfect. Handmade wrapping paper. Florentine-style marbleized paper in brilliant swirls of turquoise and emerald green. A work of art in itself, something his brilliant wife probably shot off casually on some morning in which she had a little spare time.

But the gift, ah. The gift was not something shot off casually. It was the work of many painstaking hours of labor that his wife had put in because . . . she loved him.

It still astonished him.

He looked down at the small square canvas.

A portrait of his hand. His right hand on a table, a small vase of flowers in the background. He stared. It was utterly perfect. He had big, strong hands and she captured that strength, the raised veins, the scars, even the yellow calluses on the side of his hand from a lifetime of karate.

His hand wasn't beautiful, but it was large and powerful and she caught that perfectly, and set it against the delicate crystal vase of flowers in the background, the flowers at the edge of maturity, just ready to drop their petals. The contrast between the powerful male hand and the delicate bouquet was stunning.

The canvas looked ancient, like some Renaissance painting by one of the old masters that had time-travelled to their home, the dark background and earth tones of his hand offsetting the pale pastels of the flowers.

He pointed to the vase of stunning flowers. "What are those, my love?"

His wife smiled. "Peonies."

They looked like roses, only fuller, even more beautiful.

And the perfect finishing touch, giving it a patina of ancient mystery—gilt flourishes around the edges, making a golden frame within the carved wooden frame. And . . . if you looked closely, the perfectly symmetrical pattern revealed itself to be tiny interlinked "d's". Her secret signal to him, the only time she allowed herself to even think his name.

Because his name wasn't Manuel Rabat, not at all.

In a previous life, what felt like a century ago, his name had been Viktor "Drake" Drakovich. A name that had been feared and envied in many places and hated everywhere.

A name that even now would bring hit men out of the woodwork if there was even a hint that he was alive. Criminals from all over the world would come crawling out from under rocks to travel to Oceania to have the privilege of killing him.

Drake had died back in New York in a conflagration, leaving his billion-dollar arms empire behind. He had no idea if someone had stepped into his shoes, and he didn't give a fuck. That was another life.

He had enough money for ten lifetimes and above all, he had Grace, who was now Victoria.

Grace—Victoria—never ever made a mistake, not even in private. She did everything she could to keep them safe.

It was only in her many stunning handmade gifts to him that she allowed herself their secret code. A tiny "d" somewhere in the gift. Sometimes it took him an hour to discover it.

"This is beautiful, darling," he said, cursing his inability to express fully what he felt. She'd created a masterpiece, something that, if it didn't go onto the wall in his study, would be in a museum.

Beautiful was a stupid word, an inadequate word, a nothing word.

But it made her glow. She smiled and kissed his temple. "You like it? Once—" That was her code word for the short time they'd lived together in his penthouse atop the Manhattan skyscraper that had gone down in flames. *Once.* "Once I saw your hand on your desk and there was a vase of flowers. Lilies of the valley because it was winter."

It had been snowing the day they made their escape. Sleet and snow falling heavily from the sky, together with shards of rotor blade from the rooftop helicopter his enemy had shot down. "I was so struck by the juxtaposition of your hand and the delicacy of the flowers, I knew I would paint it one day." She kissed him again. "So happy birthday, darling."

Happy birthday.

Drake had no idea whether December 23rd was his birthday or not. It had been on the passport of one of his identities while operating in West Africa as a Belgian, Hugo Van Hoof, and he'd simply retained it.

Who knew what day he'd been born? Or even what year? His earliest memories were of being a street rat on the streets of Odessa. He had no idea who his parents had been.

"My birthday," he said sourly. "And now Christmas is coming up."

She laughed because she knew perfectly well why the idea of Christmas coming up made him so exasperated. Because she'd give him a perfect Christmas present, something so unusual he wouldn't even think of needing it until she gave it to him and he'd give her—what?

It's not as if he didn't have the money to buy her things. He could probably buy her a whole country if she wanted one, albeit a small one. Maybe Andorra? Liechtenstein?

He could buy her furs, diamonds, Valentino dresses. By the ton. Chanel handbags and Gucci shoes, by the truckload. Cashmere scarves, gold-plated golf clubs, a collection of gold Rolexes. A diamond as big as the fucking Ritz.

She didn't want them.

As a matter of fact, in an attempt to keep them low profile, she specifically kept their spending down. *His* spending down because she spent almost nothing.

Every single one of the many presents she'd made him had

cost very little except time and work; they had been infused with her talent and love for him and were absolutely priceless.

The thing was, Drake was very smart. He knew how to handle money, he knew how to handle weapons, he had run a fucking empire single-handedly. He could defeat more or less any man on earth in close quarter combat.

But he didn't have a creative bone in his body, not one. When he tried to think of making her a present instead of going out and buying the most expensive thing he could, he drew a complete blank. He loved her as he had never loved another human being; she was his life, his heart, but he couldn't think of anything to get her that was an expression of his creativity, which was nonexistent, and not his bank account, which was considerable.

She wasn't in any way interested in his bank account, which still astonished him.

"Come." Grace—in his head he would always think of her as Grace—pulled at his hand. "Come look at the table I set for your first- ever birthday party."

First-ever birthday party.

It was true. The thought of organizing a birthday party had never even crossed his mind. And if it had, he'd never had friends before to celebrate with. Only employees and enemies.

Grace had changed that, too. She'd invited his airline's chief pilot and his girlfriend his driver—who was also her bodyguard though he'd never tell her that,—the mayor of Malua, their new home, and his wife. Plus the president of their bank who already thought Drake walked on water after he deposited one one-thousandth of his assets into the bank.

She'd also invited the manager of the art gallery she'd set up in town and his partner.

Acquaintances. Maybe—who knew? Maybe someday friends. As a matter of fact, without realizing it, they were becoming friends. This had never happened to him before.

The notion felt odd to him, like a new taste. He didn't even know if he liked the idea of having friends. He only knew he didn't *not* like it.

And the thought seemed to please Grace, so that was that.

He'd rarely if ever allowed men into his home, and only after passing three layers of security. He couldn't do that to people Grace had invited to celebrate his birthday, though he'd tried to suggest . . . but then Grace put her foot down.

Their guests were coming in through the front door without being patted down or passing through a metal detector. So dictated Grace Law, which was the law of his land.

Still . . . trust but verify as they said. The door frame of the entrance *was* a hidden metal detector that gave off a vibration to his cell phone instead of an auditory signal. He had security guards stationed discreetly, two of whom would be serving drinks on the patio.

Other guards were posted in hidden stations in their extensive garden and on the floor below.

And anyway, Drake had a sixth and even a seventh sense for who might be carrying in his presence. Guns and weapons had been his entire life up until very recently. He'd be willing to bet his life—and more importantly Grace's life—that he could spot a hidden weapon.

"Close your eyes." Grace smiled at his expression, reached

out with index finger and thumb and closed his eyelids. "Come on. I have something to show you."

"Another gift?" he asked in dismay. God. Already the painting was perfect. He couldn't stand *another* perfect gift.

"Not really a gift." Drake couldn't see her, but he knew his wife so very well and he knew exactly what her expression was. Loving, smiling, just a little bit exasperated at her husband who was so competent in so many ways and yet a failure at so many things ordinary people instinctively knew how to do. "Give me your hand."

He held his hand out and she took it gently, then tugged. "Come with me. No peeking."

He resisted for just a second. Giving up control to another human being went against every instinct he had. All of his life had been spent under the constant threat of violence. He was alive today because he had taken an inborn paranoia and turned it into a science. Otherwise that first assassination attempt in Kiev fifteen years ago would have got him, not to mention the twenty others over the years.

He was alive because he trusted no one.

He trusted Grace. With his life. It still gave him cognitive dissonance.

She loved him and she'd saved his life back in New York. The fact that she loved him was proved to him a thousand times a day.

The imperative—*trust no one!*—vied briefly and violently with the other imperative—*trust Grace!*—and trusting Grace won, as it always did. But it took a second to overcome long-ingrained instincts.

He was certain that Grace was standing there, patiently waiting while he violently and silently fought with himself, a scenario she'd seen dozens of times over.

To anyone who hadn't lived as Drake did, alone in the midst of the most violent criminals on earth, he must seem crazy. But Grace understood him, understood him down to his bones.

And loved him, notwithstanding the darkness and danger she knew lurked right underneath his surface.

It never failed to baffle him and thrill him.

"Okay," he said and heard her exhale.

She led him through a couple of rooms and stopped on what he knew was the threshold of the dining room. There was, as always throughout the house, a delightful scent of living plants, fresh flowers, lemons, and in this room, delicious food.

"Open your eyes, my love," Grace said.

His eyes popped open and he stared.

A fairyland. She'd turned the room into a fairyland, touched by magic. The room glowed with candles, candles everywhere, on every surface. Last year she'd learned how to make candles from a book and instead of producing lopsided messes as anyone else would, she produced a series of gorgeous candles that looked like flowers, candles with bits of seashell or flowers pressed into them, or twisting, sinuous, very modern elegant shapes that caught the eye.

Four huge candle-pillars were in the four corners, looking like alabaster, glowing from within. He had no idea how she'd made candles that big.

Their dining table was long. Down the center she'd cut supple branches and braided them all the length of the table, tall slender columns of wax placed in the interstices of the candles.

The centerpiece was a huge green Christmas tree candle with red hanging decorations.

The napkins were arranged in some amazingly complex way to look like flowers in the middle of the plates.

There was an incredibly fresh smell to the air as well, coming mainly from the open sliding doors leading out onto a patio and the swimming pool.

He had nearly lost his calm when she explained what she wanted in their new home. Open doors? Insane.

He'd spent his entire adult life behind the strongest walls and doors science could devise. An *open* door? So enemies could just walk in?

Drake was hard-wired by this point to give Grace what she wanted but this went against everything he knew about the world.

In the end, of course, he caved, but not before secretly creating a force field of security around the sprawling home on a bluff overlooking the ocean. He had 400 motion sensors and an array of IR cameras everywhere. If a fly shat on his property, or in a buffer zone of 100 meters around his property, he knew about it.

Still.

He looked out the open window, looked longingly at the sliders against the wall, his hands itching to close them . . .

"Relax," his love murmured, rubbing his back, and he did.

"Old habits, dusch—" She lay a finger against his mouth, a slight frown between her eyebrows and she shook her head slightly.

"People are coming," she said quietly.

Of course. Manuel Rabat, a Maltese businessman who'd spent time in America, would never say the Russian term of endearment *duschka*.

"Darling," he finished and she smiled and kissed him. Just a brush of her lips and all those unsettled . . . things inside him that baffled him and kept him off balance suddenly settled and focused and burned brightly with the desire he felt for his wife.

He didn't know what to do with the other emotions—and even acknowledging that he had emotions felt odd and jangled—but, by God, he knew what to do with this.

He fisted his hand in her soft, thick hair and deepened the kiss, everything roiling inside him suddenly still, focused like a diamond point on her, her mouth . . .

Drake was taking her down to the floor when a bell rang faintly.

One of their guests, otherwise he'd have been notified by his security staff.

Grace pulled away smiling, leaned her forehead against his. "Our guests are arriving."

"Yes." Kissing her was the only thing that could possibly make him forget that strangers—and the whole world was full of strangers as far as he was concerned—were coming to his door. Invited by him. Greeted as guests, allowed free rein of his home.

It still felt so foreign to him.

And then Drake watched Grace's face and saw something, something she forgot to hide from him. She wanted this evening. She wanted company and conversation.

He knew she hid her real feelings about the way they had to live, while reassuring him over and over that he was enough for her. That the world didn't matter.

But it did.

Sivuatu was paradise on earth in terms of weather and nature, but there was no cultural life, none. He knew that back in New York, she'd gone to almost every single concert in Lincoln Center, buying tickets that cost $25 and were up in the nosebleed sections because she had little money, but she was there. She went to all the plays in Central Park and to all the off-Broadway plays she could afford.

There was absolutely nothing like that here.

They lived in isolation, because of his paranoia. Absolutely justified paranoia, true, but limiting nonetheless.

Grace filled her life well. She spent her days painting and had thrown herself into gardening. Plants were one thing Sivuatu excelled at. She looked and acted happy.

But then she loved him and would never, ever complain. He knew her well enough to know that.

Right now, she was really looking forward to having guests. She'd enjoyed decorating the dining room. It was clear in the loving care she'd taken. She found pleasure in this evening.

So whatever it cost him in terms of peace of mind, it was worth it. His wife needed the world, or at least the tiny corner of it he felt safe to give her.

That was when the plan sprang full blown in his head. The *perfect* gift for Grace. And he could arrange it tonight!

The mayor and his wife were entering, smiling, looking around in awe. Smiling at Grace. Smiling at *him*.

Drake walked forward to greet them, wondering if this was going to become a new style of life.

Wondering whether he'd pay for it with his life.

"**W**ell." Grace—now Victoria—laid her hand on her husband's shoulder after their guests had gone. Even now that she'd touched him a million times, it still thrilled her to feel him under her fingers.

The first time she'd touched him it had been like laying her fingers against a powerful engine, an extraordinary feeling of sheer power under her fingertips, and it was still that way.

Her husband swung his face to hers, placing his huge hand over hers. "Well."

Grace studied his face. As usual, it gave little away. Her husband had learned to school his expressions in very harsh places. "Your first birthday party. What did you think? It wasn't so bad, was it?"

"No." He gave out a little half puff of surprise, frowning. "No, it wasn't."

"And you actually enjoyed yourself, didn't you? I saw a couple of smiles break out. Surprised the hell out of me." Her husband had a bleak and dark view of life and she was making it her life's work to slowly ease some joy and light into it.

His eyes widened, "I smiled?" She understood his surprise. Smiles were rare for him.

"Oh yeah." She kissed him. "Real, actual smiles. Lips upturned and everything. They made you very handsome. I saw the mayor's wife do a double take."

"Now, that's not possible, dusch—" He stopped, shook his head, corrected himself. "Darling. I'm as ugly as sin now. You saw to that."

She hadn't seen to it so much as overseen it. A brilliant plastic surgeon had altered the major points on his face to avoid being detected by facial recognition software. He had a flatter nose now, a slightly different chin, his stark features a little more ordinary.

"Absolutely not. You could never be ugly." The smile that had been lurking broke free. "I'm so glad you had a good time, though you were so very vigilant, always. Were you expecting someone to pull out a gun and start shooting between the sea bream and the lemon sherbet?"

It wouldn't have surprised her husband if someone had. That much she knew. He was ready for anything. A hint of unexpected violence and her husband would react instantly.

He shrugged. "Actually, the dinner party was delightfully gunshot-free. And everyone had a good time."

He still seemed a little surprised at that. Grace knew that there had been almost no social events in his previous life. Any dinners with other people had been business, mainly with criminals and outlaws, and then only when his business partners insisted. Drake said he hated negotiating at the table. He'd had dinner with his lovers, but that was different.

He'd been extremely open with her about his copious sex life before meeting her, just as he'd made it abundantly clear that that part of his life was forever over.

"Of course they had a good time. You're a fascinating man and—"

"No, darling." He kissed her forehead, looking much

more sure of himself now. "They had a good time because you created such an elegant setting, the food was fabulous, and you are a charming hostess. You put everyone at ease. A wild boar would relax at a dinner party you'd organized."

Grace smiled. It was true—to her astonishment. Being able to put people at ease was this strange new ability that had just . . . materialized.

She'd spent her entire life feeling completely estranged from everyone—an alien in human skin. A struggling artist in a world that cares nothing for art, incapable of playing the games other New Yorkers found so integral to their lives.

Somehow, Drake had changed all that. He loved her as a woman and an artist, loved her exactly as she was, and it was as if his love had shattered iron shackles, setting her free. She found it easy to relate to people now, even though she and Drake led very private lives.

"We didn't have wild boars," she chided gently.

Though judging by his wariness that first hour, there might as well have been. Drake had been stiff and formal, and the whites of his eyes had shown. He'd all but rolled them in his head like a pony's sighting a rattlesnake. Then he'd settled down. Had actually disappeared with his chief pilot for half an hour. She'd suspected them of smoking a cigar but they passed the sniff test.

She stroked his shoulder. "We had perfectly nice people over for dinner with no agenda other than to have a good time. And—" she dropped the little bomblet casually, "become friends with us. With you."

Her husband was the most controlled of men. If she hadn't had her hands actually on his shoulder, she wouldn't have noticed the little jolt at the word *friends*. The notion of having friends was still something that rocked his world.

She nuzzled his neck, never tiring of the feel of him.

They'd met in violence and tragedy. He'd killed four men under her eyes before she knew his name. But from the first moment, he'd thrown a mantle of protection over her. Though he looked frightening and *was* frightening, he'd never frightened her. Not for a second.

She would never tell him and was ashamed to admit it, even to herself, but she'd fallen in love with him the instant she'd seen him. She'd been taken at gunpoint to the alleyway outside a gallery showing her paintings and had seen a powerful man, not tall but immensely broad. He was facing three armed thugs and he hadn't looked frightened at all.

He'd looked dangerous.

And she'd fallen.

But that was another time and another continent and another life. She shivered, as if to shake the memories off.

Her husband was uncannily perceptive. "What's the matter, my love?" he asked gently.

Grace didn't answer, but turned the question around. "What were you and Mike doing when you were gone so long? Were you smoking cigars? That's what I suspected but you didn't smell of cigar smoke. Were you smoking?"

She fisted her hands on her hips and tried to look ferocious.

Her amazing husband, the strongest man she'd ever seen, a man who could never be bested in combat, a man who could outshoot any sniper, threw up his hands in mock terror.

"Never!" He gave an exaggerated shiver. "Would I risk

your wrath? I tremble at your feet. You barely let me eat meat. God only knows what the punishment would be for smoking a cigar!"

Grace narrowed her eyes. "If I caught you smoking a cigar, my revenge would be swift and merciless."

"Voilà!" he cried. His dark eyes gleamed. "Behold an obedient, completely smoke-free husband!"

She laughed. Getting him to eat a healthy diet was an ongoing struggle. In New York he'd lived like the Sun King and had eaten like the Sun King, too. He'd had a rotating staff of top chefs on the floor below his penthouse and they sent up elaborate four-star meals three times a day that were the equivalent of mainlining cholesterol.

Now she fed him fish and fruits and vegetables and he grumbled about having to obey the food police, but she knew he was feeling better.

"So, don't change the subject. Where did you two go off to?"

This time the smile was sly. "Ah, my darling. I went off to arrange . . . your Christmas present."

Grace's eyes rolled as she stifled a sigh. The eternal question. What could he give her? He asked her that a thousand times a day, and at each birthday, Valentine's Day, Christmas, he visibly suffered.

What could he give her?

Nothing.

She had everything she could possibly desire. A husband who loved her and whose love was made visible and tangible every second of every day. A beautiful home on a tropical island. Time and space to paint.

What else could she possibly want or need?

Certainly not the expensive baubles he kept trying to give her.

"Not another diamond?" she asked suspiciously. The last one was so big it weighed down her hand and nearly blinded her whenever they were in sunshine, which was every day in Sivuatu. After a week, it went back into its box and into a wall safe that held about a hundred of its kin.

He laughed. "You are perhaps the only woman in the world who doesn't want diamonds, my beloved. Actively dislikes them."

"I don't *dislike* them," Grace murmured.

Diamonds were rocks. Big, shiny rocks whose only purpose was to attract a huge amount of attention. A woman draped in expensive jewelry was the object of envy, sometimes hatred. The opposite of what they needed. To save their lives, they needed to fly under everyone's radar.

Drake realized in theory but not in practice that ordinariness was a protective cloak around them, one she tried to pull over them at every opportunity.

Being ordinary protected them. In New York, Drake had lived large, albeit away from prying eyes, but with an outrageous degree of luxury. And all the tight security in the world, the armed guards and bulletproof windows hadn't been enough to save him because his enemies knew he was there.

They'd gone to a great deal of trouble and effort to convince his enemies that he was dead. So why attract attention with an outrageously fancy home, high living, jewels, and super expensive designer clothes?

It was insane, suicidal.

"Diamonds attract attention, and we don't want that, my love." She twined her arms around his neck and kissed him just below the ear, a spot she knew from experience would make him shudder.

Ah, yes.

"I don't need diamonds," she whispered in his ear. "I need you."

He had his arm around her waist, holding her tightly to him and she felt him rise urgently against her stomach.

To her surprise, instead of taking her down to the ground, or over to the sofa, he stepped away with a secretive smile.

"So. All right." His voice had that slight guttural tone of arousal and she could *see* how sexually excited he was. Nonetheless, he kept himself out of arm's reach and handed her three sheets of paper. "Here's your Christmas present, two days early."

Puzzled, she took the sheets, reading carefully, not understanding until—all of a sudden—she understood.

Her eyes widened as she lifted them to her husband in shock. He was smiling. "Are these—" she held up the sheets of perfectly ordinary photocopy paper. "Are these for real? For—for us?"

"Oh yes," he answered softly. "In another name, of course."

"Of course."

They'd had several identities since their "death," and continued to have them. For example, she ordered hard copy books from Amazon to be delivered to Australia, then flown in to their island by her husband's airline under one fictitious name and credit card, and ebooks set up on her Kindle account under another fictitious name and fictitious credit card.

"These are—" All of a sudden her hands shook, the paper rattling. "These are tickets to *Aida* at the Sydney Opera House, to a showing of *Phantom of the Opera* and to a showing of *Cirque du Soleil*," she whispered. "All in Sydney."

"They are all right?" Drake asked suddenly with a frown. "On the website it said that there were live elephants onstage at the *Aida*. I don't know what that means. Who wants live elephants on a stage? Imagine if they have a bowel movement? And the other shows—apparently they are very popular. These are things you would like to see?"

"Very much," she assured him softly.

"And there is a show of 100 Picassos at the Museum of Sydney. I know you'll like that."

Grace was as tempted as she had ever been in her life. Diamonds didn't tempt her, not in any way, but *this*. An opera, two shows. *Picassos*. Her voice trembled as much as her hands as she put the printouts of the ticket reservations down, trying to conceal her sadness.

"My love, I can't accept these. I won't endanger us. It's not worth it."

They had to stay on this island forever. Drake had made that clear when they escaped the assassination attempt and made their way here to Sivuatu.

He bought the airline company flying into and out of the island and the three shipping companies whose ships docked here. He knew everyone who came to the island and surreptitiously recorded their faces. He had his finger on the pulse of the island, no question.

This island was safe.

He was shaking his head. "How can you imagine, my

dusch—my darling, that I wouldn't think this through? I never operated in Oceania, never. I never even operated in southeast Asia. I cannot imagine any of my old enemies in Australia. We will fly over under assumed names on SivAir's executive jet. I have arranged for us to rent a private apartment in downtown Sydney so we won't need to check into a hotel. Australia has very few CCTVs on its city streets, much fewer than, say, London or Paris or New York. When we are outside, we will wear big straw hats and sunglasses. For the shows, I bought us box seats and bought all the other tickets in the box."

She laughed. "Of course you did."

A faint tendril of hope made its way to her heart.

"And while making the arrangements, I had no pickle. No pickle at all."

"Pickle?"

"Pickle of danger."

She forced herself not to smile, ruthlessly beat down the laugh. "No . . . pickle of danger?" The laugh lay treacherously in wait in her throat. She had a sudden image of him in one of his martial arts stances, brandishing . . . a pickle.

"Not one," he said seriously. "I have a finely honed sense of danger, perfected over a lifetime, and I am feeling nothing at the thought of us going to Sydney for three days."

She blinked at him, hardly daring to hope that this would happen.

"So." He picked up the show and opera tickets and handed them back to her. She took them with shaking hands. "Do you honestly feel I would endanger us? That I wouldn't plan this carefully?"

"I don't know." She searched his eyes. "I don't know how far you'd go to please me. It frightens me because it's not necessary. You keep harping on wanting to get me nice presents, simply because I make a few things for you by hand."

"You make me masterpieces. Priceless works of art. But much as I love to please you, you don't think I would endanger you needlessly, do you?"

Put that way . . . "No."

"So." It was his favorite word. He had the faintest traces of an accent. He'd grown up an orphan on the streets of Odessa. In his previous incarnation as the head of a huge crime syndicate, he spoke five languages perfectly and another five well enough to negotiate. His English was nearly perfect and the slight accent bothered no one in Sivuatu as they expected a Maltese man to have an accent.

But she found it so sexy when he said "so." Drawing the word out. *Zooo.*

"So. We are going. We will spend Christmas among the throngs in Sydney, seeing shows and Picassos and, God help me, an opera." This last said with a painful wince and she laughed. "Are you happy?"

He'd done this for her. How could she not be happy?

"Oh yes. Incredibly, wildly happy." She was studying the tickets, imagining *Aida* and the *Cirque*. And the *Phantom*! All those years in New York and stupidly, she'd never gone, though she loved the CD and knew the songs by heart. She stared at the white mask with the red rose logo.

"And are you grateful?"

"Oh yes," she answered dreamily, thinking of the three days ahead of them.

"*How* grateful?" She looked up in surprise at the suddenly harsh, hoarse tone.

And blushed.

They had a fabulous sex life. Drake was an attentive, tender lover who took his time in pleasing her. But every once in a while something in him changed and she caught a glimpse of the truly dangerous man he really was. She hadn't tamed him, not one bit. He just chose to show her a tender side he said he'd only discovered with her.

But sometimes the tiger in him growled and clawed its way to the surface. And then the sex was incandescent.

His entire body was tense, tendons standing out on his strong neck, huge hands flexed. Those dark brown eyes glowed as if there were a power source inside him that had suddenly roared to life. As she watched, a huge shudder went through him. "I said—how grateful?"

Watching his transformation was amazing but even more amazing was what happened to her in those moments.

Something—something *animal* in her awoke, too.

A flush of extreme heat washed over her, head to toes, the heat fizzing under her skin, glowing between her thighs. She could barely breathe, barely form the words.

"Very." Her throat was tight, almost closed. Speaking was hard because speaking wasn't what she wanted to do. "Very grateful."

They weren't touching but it was as if a red-hot flaming rod connected them. She could see his arousal even without looking down at his groin. It was in his face, the flush over those high cheekbones with a hint of Tartar blood, the tight mouth, flared nostrils.

And he could see hers, too. She had very pale skin that showed most emotions. Now it would be flushed. Sweat broke out on her back, a drop curled between her breasts.

"Show me," he whispered darkly. "Show me how grateful you are."

"Okay," she whispered back.

Driven by something entirely beyond her control, Grace took her clothes off. Slowly. Not because she wanted to entice him with some kind of striptease—when he was like this, he needed no enticement—but because her hands shook and her knees felt so weak they could hardly keep her upright. She had to move slowly or she'd fall down in a puddle of heat.

Or blow up.

Thick bands of steel encircled her chest, making it hard to breathe. Spots swam in front of her eyes.

With trembling hands, she reached to the side. Her dress was held at the waist with a small sash anchored by a bow. She undid it and the two panels fell open. Underneath was a strapless bra and panties. She did indulge in expensive underwear, because it couldn't be seen and because it turned on her husband.

He was massively turned on now. She could almost see the waves of arousal coming off him like smoke. He nearly vibrated with desire.

"Off. Dress."

Now she knew how aroused he was because he was losing his faculty of speech. And syntax.

Slowly, she pulled the emerald green linen sheath off her shoulders, letting the dress fall to the floor.

His eyes flared and he waved his hand impatiently at her.

Deep breath. His big hand had all but sent waves of heat her way, hitting her groin like bolts of fire.

She reached behind her, unsnapped her bra. The light silk fluttered to the floor. At any other moment, she'd have admired the pale green silk on the dark emerald green linen, but her brain was too blasted to notice aesthetic niceties. All she felt was heat turning her bones liquid.

"Panties," he said, his voice guttural. His dark eyes studied every aspect of her body so intensely it was as if he were touching her instead of watching her.

Panties. Oh God. Taking off her panties was going to require balance and her legs could barely hold her. She gripped the edge of the chest of drawers with one hand, while pulling down her panties with the other. They, too, fluttered softly down to land around her ankles.

"Off."

Still gripping the corner of the chest of drawers, she lifted one sandaled foot, then the other. While he watched, one foot nudged the soft silk panties over to the pile of clothes.

She was naked and about ready to fall over.

Drake didn't move. He simply watched her with molten eyes, still fully dressed.

"Do you want me?" he asked hoarsely.

"You have no idea," Grace whispered.

"Show me."

Show him?

She looked down at herself. Her nipples were hard, cherry-red. Her left breast fluttered with her pounding heartbeat. Of course, he couldn't see her liquid knees, couldn't feel how tight her chest was.

There was only one other thing she could show him.

Grace parted her legs, one knee slightly bent. Looking down, the angle was wrong for her, but surely he could see the lips of her sex glistening? With her legs spread, the air felt cool on her wet sex.

"Show me more," he insisted.

O-kay.

Still gripping the corner with white fingers, Grace ran her free hand slowly down the center of her body. Her skin felt hot to the touch, slightly damp. One finger between her breasts, then the flat of her palm over her belly.

Drake's gaze followed her hotly, riveted on her hand.

When she stopped her hand along her lower belly, his gaze snapped up to hers.

He didn't even talk, just jerked his head downward.

More.

She nodded jerkily.

They were both beyond words now.

Grace opened her hand and slid it between her legs, closing her eyes as she touched herself. She needed Drake's touch, she craved it, her vagina wept for it. At least her fingers quenched the red-hot heat, if only a little.

She ran her index and middle fingers along the lips of her sex and moaned a soft exhale of breath.

Drake shuddered again, throughout his entire body.

Slowly, because if she moved quickly, her legs would give way, Grace slid her middle finger inside her and breathed out again in a harsh gasp, as if she'd been hurt.

It wasn't pain she was feeling.

Drake moaned too.

She slid her finger out a little, then back in. It wasn't anything like feeling her husband's member inside her, but it was something. Anything was better than this empty, hungry heat that cried for his touch.

When she slid her finger back in, her vagina clenched around it, hard. Her legs instinctively tightened, her stomach muscles pulled.

She looked down, saw it, looked up at her husband. He saw it too. Her hand slid away and she showed it to him. The palm of her hand and especially her middle finger coated with her juices.

She licked her middle finger.

It was as if he suddenly burst free of restraints. He lunged for her, pulled her against him while somehow, at the same time, freeing himself, pulling his huge, erect penis out from his pants.

With one arm her husband, the strongest man she'd ever seen, lifted her up, settling her legs around his waist, and entered her with one hard thrust.

They were kissing wildly and they both exhaled as he pushed hard into her.

With no effort whatsoever, one hand behind her head, the other holding her by the hips, Drake walked them to the bed.

Every step moved him inside her, inside her highly sensitized tissues, even the slight movements almost as exciting as his thrusts.

She was whimpering by the time he reached their huge bed. Bending over slowly, still embedded inside her, he gently placed her back on the bedspread and sprawled on top of her.

When bending, she could feel the iron-hard muscles of his stomach against hers through his silk shirt.

It was exciting, being completely naked against him, his penis deep inside her, while he was fully dressed. She could feel the unyielding muscles of his back and shoulders under the silk shirt against the inside of her arms, the back of his hard thighs, encased in the polished cotton pants, against her legs.

She felt completely open, completely vulnerable to this hard, tough, highly dangerous man who would never hurt her.

His penis was like a hard, hot club inside her.

He was huge. When they made love, his foreplay lasted forever because he wanted to make sure she could take him without pain. He'd been able to enter her in one stroke only because she'd been so excited and so very wet.

She pulsed around him, another hard pull of her vagina and he winced.

"Not yet, my love."

The words ran around her empty head, not making much sense. But there was only one answer to her husband. "Okay," she panted.

Grace lifted herself, eyes closing as she felt him lengthen even further, something that should have been impossible. Already it felt as if he were reaching up into her heart.

She pulsed around him again and felt him jerk inside her.

"Wait!" He moved around on top of her doing something that pushed him even further inside her.

A shoe thumped on the floor, coupled with a huge thump

of her heart. Her entire body stilled, centered totally on where he was inside her, so hot and heavy.

Moving on her, in her, another thump and she exploded in a climax, writhing under him, clinging to him with her arms and legs as she clenched around him explosively, pulling hard on his penis with her internal muscles.

Her back arched and sounds came out of her mouth, animal sounds, sounds almost of pain while the firebomb of heat kept her pulsing against him, clenching rhythmically, shaking with the intensity of it.

Finally, the pulses died down, became less intense, less on the knife's edge of pain. Became a sensual pleasure, like rocking on an endless warm ocean. And then stopped.

She was coated with sweat from head to toe, utterly incapable of thought, incapable even of directing her muscles. Her arms fell to her sides, her legs opened, no longer able to cling to his hips.

She relaxed utterly, rocking on that endless ocean, simply breathing and enjoying the aftershocks of intense please.

Finally, she was able to open her eyes, only to find his dark brown eyes staring into hers from less than an inch away. He was so close she could feel the wash of his breath over her face.

He smiled, a slow curling of his lips that made her toes curl.

"Ah, my love. If you climaxed that hard when I took off my shoes, what's going to happen when I take off my pants?"

Sydney, Australia
The next day

Drake stood at the huge picture window of the luxury penthouse apartment he'd rented. It had been expensive, but that was nothing. As a matter of fact, if this trip went well, and Grace enjoyed herself, there might be other trips to Sydney and he would buy this apartment or one like it.

They wouldn't come often. It is not good to tempt fate, as the Americans said. Maybe twice a year. He could just buy this flat under an assumed name and keep it for their use.

Because, well, Grace was excited and happy, and next to keeping her safe, that was his priority.

The apartment wasn't a fortress like his penthouse in Manhattan had been. The windows weren't bullet-resistant, as they had been in Manhattan. The truth was, though, that with all his security in Manhattan—the armed guards 24/7, the elaborate electronic sensor system, the bulletproof windows—it hadn't been enough to keep him safe.

The assassin's attack had almost taken his life and would have if not for Grace, who'd saved him.

New York had been dangerous for him in a way Sydney was not.

New York was a nexus for the kind of men who bought what he had had to sell. No doubt there was some kind of arms trade in Sydney but it was small scale and didn't involve the major global players. He should know. He'd been at the top of the pile.

He looked out over the exquisite harbor, the brilliant setting sun painting everything with a vivid glow, bringing out the intense colors of the ocean, the light reflecting like diamonds off the many beautiful buildings.

Seeing things from an aesthetic point of view was new. It was his curse and his pleasure, and entirely Grace's fault. All his life, it had never occurred to him to look at things and see their beauty. All he had ever done was scan his environment for threats and, God knows, there had been enough of them.

Threats.

He sent out his senses, reviewed the situation. They'd flown over in his company's private jet. They'd entered the country under different identities, he'd rented the apartment in the name of a shell corporation that could never be traced back to any specific human being, and the tickets had been bought in the name of yet another identity.

They'd worn broad-brimmed straw hats and large sunglasses from the airport to the apartment, which was perfectly plausible since it was nearly 100 degrees outside.

Heat at Christmas. He'd spent his entire life in the Northern Hemisphere with the exception of two visits to Johannesburg. A balmy Christmas season still surprised him.

It had been 92 degrees in Sivuatu when they'd left.

He admired the scenery while continuing to scan for threats, but nothing pinged his radar.

Of course, it was perfectly possible that his radar had been permanently ruined by the most frightening emotion known to man—happiness.

Happiness could kill him.

Happiness terrified him and fascinated him. He'd never been happy in his previous life. Though he'd been the top player in a dangerous game for a very long time, his ascent there had been brutal and he'd had to remain vigilant every second of every day to stay alive on the top of that heap.

What he'd had had seemed enough. Power and the luxuries money could buy.

But then, of course, there was the blood price to be paid—hatred and fear and envy. Murderous rage. Men on three continents whose only thought was to assassinate him and take his place.

Vigilance was in his DNA, but he'd had little reason to exercise it since he'd died and started his new life with Grace.

Was he getting soft?

He mulled that over. A safe life, someone to love . . . would that be his downfall? Men had been known to grow soft, lose their edge, and then their life.

He searched inside himself carefully because he was betting not only his life but Grace's.

No. Certitude settled in his chest. They were safe. This could be done. This might even be the new normal.

A safe, happy life with the woman he loved. Unthinkable before now.

"Darling?"

Drake whirled and his heart turned over in his chest. How could that be? They'd been together a year. He'd had her hundreds of times. He knew her body and her soul inside out. And yet, there it was.

When he saw her unexpectedly, his heart would give this huge thump in his chest like a heart attack, only not. He knew because he'd gone to a cardiologist and had his heart checked. The doctor had smiled and said he would live to be a hundred.

It was Grace who did this to him.

There she was, in a beautiful dress she'd had made from a bolt of pale turquoise Chinese silk her seamstress's son had sent from Shanghai. It had cost practically nothing. The seamstress was superb but inexpensive.

Grace had made her own jewelry—glass beads with intricate swirls of color strung on strands of silk. She had a cream shawl in case the air turned chilly later on, simple sandals, a simple small black purse. Her entire outfit cost about half what he usually spent on wine at dinner with one of his mistresses back in Manhattan and she looked like a million dollars.

"You look beautiful," he said softly and she looked up at him in surprise.

His entire body felt on edge, skin too tight to contain it.

"Thank you," his love said with a smile. She walked up to him and touched his cheek. He covered her hand with his and brought her hand to his mouth. He touched his tongue to her palm and watched her pupils dilate.

Ah, yes. She felt it, too.

Grace stepped back sharply, as if against a magnetic current.

She shook her head. "I know what you're thinking. And much as I'd like to play with you, we have reservations for dinner and the opera."

"Yes, ma'am." With some difficulty, Drake reined himself in. Over the course of the past year, he'd grown used to having Grace whenever he wanted. There had never been any constraints other than if she was feeling desire or not.

She felt desire right now, it was clear. A faint rose under her light tan, breathing irregular and fast. Oh yes, she desired him too.

But he *could* have her, any time he wanted. It would be selfish of him to indulge himself now and miss the dinner date, when dinner and the theater were his Christmas gifts to her.

Drake had a great deal of control over his body. He'd held perfectly still while a bone had been set and stitches had been taken without anesthesia. He could deal with the tiny bite of deferred lust.

He held out his arm like the gentleman he wasn't.

"Ma'am? I thought we'd walk to the restaurant. It isn't far."

He enjoyed the inrush of breath, the blinding smile she turned up at him, the blush of joy. "We can walk to the restaurant? That would be wonderful. It's a beautiful evening. But—but is it safe?"

For the millionth time, Drake realized what he'd asked of Grace. To give up almost everything for him. She'd told him she used to love taking long walks around Manhattan. They hadn't gone for a walk—a real walk—since they escaped the assassination attempt over a year ago.

He tucked a shiny red-brown lock of hair behind her ear and bent to kiss her cheek. "We can walk."

They took the elevator down and plunged into the happy Christmas crowds on the street. Grace's head was swiveling to catch everything. He knew she was storing up images, colors, shapes, and nuances of light.

His head wasn't swiveling but he was alert. They walked a pedestrian street filled with happy crowds. Some kids were breakdancing and they stopped to watch. They were very good, a delight to watch. Fluid and lithe, awash in the joy of youth and health. Unobtrusively, Drake let an Australian hundred dollar bill flutter into the silk top hat on the ground.

"Your spidey sense telling you everything is okay?" Grace's amused voice sounded behind him.

He turned to meet her smiling eyes. "Hmm? My spidey sense?"

Grace laughed, hooked her arm through his again. "Obviously, your knowledge of pop culture is deficient. It comes from Spiderman. He has a spider's senses, greater than ours. Your pickle."

He looked down at her and she laughed again, elbowing him in the side. "Your pickle? Of awareness?"

"Oh." Drake looked around as they walked. No, strolled. *Strolled*. To his certain knowledge, he'd never walked slowly through any city, enjoying the sights. And for the last ten years of his criminal career, he'd never walked at all, but had himself driven from point A to point B in an armored Mercedes with tinted windows and its own air supply. Cut off from the world in a steel cocoon of safety.

Never, ever like this—alive to all the sights and sounds and smells of a great city.

He expanded his awareness. He had a highly refined sense of danger, born of a lifetime of battle. An entire lifetime where a moment's inattention, underestimating an adversary, not noticing the details of a hidden threat could get him killed.

Danger usually manifested in a sense of dread, a tingling at the nape of his neck, cold in the pit of his stomach.

Nothing. He was feeling absolutely nothing like that. No coldness, no darkness. No threat. Just happy human beings as far as the eye could see. Some were hurrying, yes, from point A to point B, but most were ambling along, looking at the brightly lit shop windows, enjoying the last of the sunshine. Many poking their heads into restaurants, planning the evening meal.

How had he missed this his entire life? All this movement and activity, sights, sounds, smells? There was a palpable essence in the air he could only ascribe to happy people all in one place and it was something he had never experienced before. Something he had never even known was possible.

"No pickle at all," he said absently. He took another sweep, encountering only people minding their own business, with no interest in him whatsoever. If anything, a couple of men took appreciative looks at Grace, then turned their heads when he stared them down.

"It's nice, isn't it?" Grace rubbed her head against his shoulder, the kind of gesture that still baffled him. A gesture of affection, totally unrelated to sex. "Being with all these happy people on a sunny day?"

"Yes, my love. It is. It is very nice."

By now Drake had grown used to Grace's uncanny understanding of his emotions. At times, she seemed to understand him better than he understood himself.

It would have frightened him, but the one thing he had come to understand this past year, the thing that now formed the bedrock of his existence, was that Grace truly loved him. He was safe in her hands, in every way.

"I checked the map. The restaurant is not far from here. And the opera is just around the corner." He gave an exaggerated shudder and Grace laughed again.

This was all so delicious. So unusual. So . . . so *new*. He was getting no danger signals at all. He saw very few security cameras and was certain that their hats and sunglasses were sufficient disguise.

So. They might be able to do this a few more times.

It would please Grace and damned if it wouldn't please him.

A quarter of an hour later, they were at the restaurant.

The restaurant was beautiful. *La Mer.* Modern fusion cuisine with French overtones, or so the restaurant site had told him. He had no idea what that meant, but the food smelled delicious.

It was a large, modern space filled with light. The entire back wall was plate glass doors looking out over the glorious harbor. The doors were open. Directly outside the doors was a long, narrow infinity pool, artfully situated so that it looked as if the edge of the pool merged with the ocean.

Instead of air-conditioning, there were big ceiling fans and an ocean breeze wafting through the room.

Waiters bustled by holding plates of food that looked like works of art. Judging from the pleased expressions of the diners, the food tasted as good as it looked.

Grace stopped on the threshold, looking around slowly. Her face glowed as she sighed with pleasure. "This is fabulous! And the food smells so good! However did you find it when you said you'd never been to Sydney before?" She smiled up at him. "What a foolish question. You Googled 'Most expensive restaurant in Sydney'."

He winced. Actually it had been "Best restaurant in Sydney" and La Mer had come up as first choice on nine out of ten lists.

He'd checked out the floor plan and the promise of an

extra 150 dollars had ensured a table at the far end of the room, close to the doors and the wonderful view.

Seated, he sat back and watched Grace order for them. He didn't care what the fuck he ate. It would be good. And it was just so wonderful watching her as she concentrated on the menu with a ferocious frown.

"I hope you like what I ordered for you," she said finally, after endless discussions with their friendly, patient waiter. It had taken Drake less time to negotiate a ten million dollar sale of arms to an Abkhazian warlord.

"All fish," he said with a sigh. He would have preferred meat, but she had him on a strict meat quota and he'd eaten his quota for the month last week. "I'm sure I'll enjoy it," he added politely. "Maybe they will have to catch the fish and it will take so long to catch it and cook it that we will be late to the opera."

She laughed and he smiled at the sound. He loved hearing her laugh.

A wine steward with spiked dyed-blond hair poured them the wine she'd ordered. A South African Chardonnay.

Delicious.

It was a sign of his ease that he would drink alcohol in public. Something he would never have done in his previous life.

That was how he was starting to think of it. A previous life. Another one entirely, not his, not any more.

This was his life now. Walking down a shopping street full of people. A delicious meal in a beautiful restaurant. Later, the opera. His pleasure dimmed a little at the thought, but who knew? Maybe the new Drake—Manuel Rabat—might actually enjoy it. He knew he'd certainly enjoy his wife's delight.

A life of—of *enjoyment*.

Unthinkable before.

Quite possible now.

The waiter slid appetizers in front of them. Fried baby octopus, oysters wrapped in prosciutto, hot clam dip. Some fish he didn't recognize with a ginger and chili sauce. Fried focaccia bread triangles with brie mousse.

"Oh God," Grace moaned as she spread the mousse and popped a focaccia in her mouth. "This is delicious!"

He would have smiled if his own mouth hadn't been full.

Grace looked around again once the appetizers were gone. "It's so strange to have all this Christmas spirit in summer. A hot weather Christmas."

It was. Jazz renditions of Christmas carols played softly in the background. A huge Christmas tree made of lit glass cylinders glowed in a corner. Palm leaves studded with tiny lights were twined around the balustrade of the iron and glass staircase leading up to a loft.

A fat Santa Claus waddled through the entrance, fake beard moving in the breeze generated by the ceiling fans.

It was Christmas but unlike any Christmas he'd ever seen. Hot and sunny. Perfect beach weather.

Australians were an informal people and most of the diners even in this expensive restaurant were in sundresses and Bermudas, with acres of suntanned skin showing.

Grace touched his hand. "We'll get used to it."

"Oh yes," he said softly.

Yes, they would. He hated the cold. He'd spent his entire

childhood on the streets of Odessa. In winter, he'd desperately tried not to freeze to death, huddling in doorways and over grates. If he was never again cold in this lifetime, he'd be a happy man.

And . . . well, he *was*. He was a happy man. The thought still stunned him.

"We can make this a Christmas tradition," he told Grace. "Christmas in Sydney. My Christmas gift to you."

"The opera," she sighed and rolled her eyes at his expression. "Verdi, Puccini, Wagner."

Drake shrugged and drank another sip of wine to help make the thought go down.

The piped-in music segued to a lovely saxophone rendering of *Do You Hear What I Hear?* One of the few carols he recognized. The soulful music, gentle and soft in the background, filled his head.

Nearby, a flame ignited at a table as the waiter threw cognac over some kind of creamy dessert and lit it. A woman at the table with the flambé dessert threw her head back and laughed.

Santa Claus was making the rounds of the tables shouting *Ho! Ho! Ho! Merry Christmas!*

The maître d'hôtel stepped away from his station frowning.

Their waiter slid a steaming oval platter of seafood risotto in front of a diner at the table next to them. Drake looked over with interest because he'd ordered it. Or rather, Grace had ordered it for him. It looked excellent and—

Ice hit his stomach.

His head lifted. He was suddenly alert.

Music, food, wine instantly forgotten.

What he was in his essence—an animal under constant threat—came instantly to the fore.

He looked carefully around the restaurant, no longer happy, no longer relaxed. If he'd been a submarine, the torpedo signal would be going off. He scanned the restaurant as a sniper would—in quadrants, careful to take in every single element.

Happy diners, innocuous-looking serving staff. A fat Santa Claus wishing everyone Merry Christmas.

What was wrong?

The frowning maître d' was conferring with the head waiter, heads together.

Drake started slowly hyperventilating. Whatever was wrong, his body knew it needed extra oxygen to deal with it.

He'd had his hand over Grace's and now removed it. He would need both hands.

Fuck. He was without weapons. He was a superb shot but he was without any firepower whatsoever. It had been an executive decision. His jet had a disassembled long gun and a Beretta in a lockbox camouflaged as a first aid kit on his jet, but he'd decided to enter Australia clean. If he bought an apartment here, he'd stock it with weapons. Just in case.

A woman laughed and clinked glasses with another woman at a table ten meters away. They were obviously celebrating something.

His stomach twisted, muscles readying themselves for action.

What was wrong?

"Ho ho ho! Merry Christmas!" the Santa Claus cried, edging his way through the tables along the wall.

The maître d' was talking into a cell phone.

"Ho ho ho! Merry Christmas!"

It was delivered in the exact tone and cadence as before.

Drake looked at the Santa Claus more closely. There was something about the tone of the voice . . . at the next *ho ho ho* he got it.

It was a recording, the words on a loop every two minutes or so. He was wearing an excellent Santa Claus outfit. Even Drake, who'd never celebrated Christmas, could see that. The suit excellently tailored, made of expensive material. Snow white, blood red. Big black belt around a huge belly.

Santa Claus was making his way around the perimeter of the room, waving his hands covered in white gloves, wishing everyone a Merry Christmas in a recorded voice on a loop.

He was coming closer to Drake's table now. Drake could observe him more clearly.

All Drake's senses went on overdrive. The smells and sounds became acute. His vision sharpened. He'd swiftly eliminated all the diners as the source of his sharp sense of danger and now focused on Santa.

The suit, the felt cap, the fake beard—they all looked very hot on this warm evening. Sweat fell down Santa's face. Taking with it pale makeup. Beneath the makeup, Santa's skin was very brown.

The sweat was removing the pale makeup entirely, falling to the red jacket in pale streaks.

Santa's belly looked lumpy, as if full of hard things and not soft stuffing.

The maître d' finished his phone call, closing the cell with a snap, and headed Santa's way.

Santa saw him coming. His dark brown eyes opened so wide the whites showed and Drake's highly evolved danger signals overloaded.

Time slowed down almost to a stop.

Santa pulled at his jacket, closed with Velcro, the ripping sound preternaturally loud to his ears.

The maître d' was twenty meters away, raising his hand to Santa, palm out. The universal stop sign.

The panels of the red Santa suit were slowly pulled apart by Santa's white-gloved hands and instead of cotton stuffing there was a vest with black cylinders attached, a string with a round pull hanging from the cylinders.

In this time out of time, Santa's hand slowly moved up to tug at the dangling string while the maître d' shouted and Drake picked up the silver charger from his table with one hand and a sharp filet knife from a nearby serving tray with the other and hurled both at Santa with all his strength.

The charger and knife slowly, slowly made their way to Santa's throat just as Santa's hand closed around the string.

"Allahu akhbar!" Santa screamed.

Again, in that slow-motion state of time during combat, as soon as the charger and knife left Drake's hands, he slashed upward, knocking over the heavy wooden table so it was between him and Santa and pulled Grace to the ground, covering as much of her as he could, while Santa fell into the infinity pool.

Then time came roaring back.

There was a huge explosion, the sound making his diaphragm vibrate. Drake hunched over Grace, wishing he could punch her into the ground to give her more protection, his arms around her head.

A red rain fell while screams started up all around them. Horribly, a severed white-gloved hand thumped to the floor an inch away from him, bouncing once then rolling away.

"Grace," he shouted above the screams, still slightly deaf from the explosion. He lifted slightly and touched her frantically all over, face, torso, legs. "Are you all right?"

She was in shock, eyes wide in a completely white face. She nodded and swallowed heavily.

He chanced a look around, taking his attention away from Grace for just a second.

The diners, so happy and content only seconds ago, were screaming and scrambling for the door, tables and chairs overturned, slipping and sliding on the platters of food that had been dashed to the floor.

The infinity pool was red, bits and pieces of human being floating to the surface.

Drake took in the situation in a flash. There was confusion and a number of people were bleeding, one woman stared at her red hand and started screaming. Several people walked around, dazed.

But there was no one on the ground in the unmistakable sprawl of death. Everything Drake saw was minor—cuts and contusions and shock. The water had absorbed most of the blast.

The only dead man was the fucker in the suicide vest and he was now safely in that special hell reserved for people who killed in the name of God.

A siren started up outside, then two.

"My darling!" Drake kissed Grace, held her tightly. He could have lost her but he hadn't. His miracle of a wife, safe.

He was trembling. Drake had spent his entire life in combat, he had learned to keep his head in combat, otherwise he'd have been long dead.

But now he trembled as he embraced his wife.

Under him, Grace stirred, her arms snaked around his neck, hanging on to him as tightly as he clung to her.

Her rapid breaths of shock sounded loud in his ear, her heart hammered against his chest.

All wonderful signs that she was alive.

She gasped, as if she'd stopped breathing, took in a huge breath that sounded like a sob.

"Drake," she whispered, and he knew how shocked she was to use the name she'd forbidden herself to ever pass her lips.

"Right here," he answered back. He kissed her temple. "It's over now. It's all right. We're fine."

Her arms tightened even more, then relaxed slightly. "Drake?"

He lifted his head, able now to smile into his wife's eyes. "Hmm?"

She drew in another breath, and let it out shakily.

"Your pickle?" Grace lifted her head and kissed him. "Best. Gift. Ever."

HOT SECRETS

Jack Prescott kissed his wife's shoulder and watched as she smiled in her sleep. That smile came from the deepest part of her and was just for him.

It still dazzled him, a year into marriage. *She* still dazzled him.

Caroline. His wife. Caroline Lake, now Caroline Prescott. The woman who'd been in his head more than half his life and now was his.

He'd showed up exactly a year ago—in her bookstore in the middle of a snowstorm—after flying nonstop for forty-eight hours from Sierra Leone. Sierra Leone had been his last mission, an homage to his dead adoptive father.

On a pirogue from Abuja to Freetown, from Lungi Airport to Paris, Paris to Atlanta, Atlanta to Seattle—and onto a tiny puddle jumper that barely made it through the wild weather, straight to Summerville. Thinking of Caroline every second of the way, the woman he'd never been able to get out of his head. While he joined the army, earned his Ranger tab, fought in innumerable hellholes throughout the world—there she'd been. Beautiful, kind, smart. The woman of any man's dreams and out of his reach throughout his twelve long, lonely years in hard and violent places.

She'd been in his head since he was a boy in a homeless shelter, bringing him books and food and a sense of the outside world, a world that didn't mean living with filthy crazies and violent drunks.

She'd been there in his head when he'd run away, was adopted by his father of the heart, Colonel Eugene Prescott. She'd been there through his deployments to bad places, trying to lend some order to a violent world. She'd been there over long, lonely nights in faraway hellholes, reminding him there was something in the world worth fighting for.

She'd been there so long, was so deeply embedded in his very soul, that when his adoptive father died and he inherited a fortune, he went back to where he'd been a lost boy and expected to find a married woman with kids—because what sane man wouldn't marry someone as beautiful and smart as Caroline?

But the world was made of wusses. Caroline had lost her parents, lost all her family money, and had looked after a badly injured younger brother for the better part of a decade—and not many men would put up with that.

He would have, no question. For Caroline he'd walk across lakes of fire, climb mountains of thorns, slay every dragon there was. Gladly. A sick brother was nothing. Plus, he had plenty of money of his own.

When he showed up on her doorstep, expecting to find a married Caroline and just wanting to see her one last time before starting the next stage of his life, it turned out she wasn't married after all and she *was* the next stage.

And he—the man who'd never had a family, the man who had known in his bones he'd never have a family because families were for other people—well, now he had a family of his own. Caroline. And the children they'd make.

At the thought of Caroline pregnant, his cock—already hard—turned to stone. A wave of heat washed over him and his breathing sped up.

It was the hardest thing about being married to Caroline. Everything else about marriage to her was incredibly easy. Intensely pleasurable. Around-the-clock delight.

She was even-tempered, without those mood swings that drove him crazy with other women. She was wicked-smart, with a sharp sense of humor. She was kind-hearted. Their home was beautiful, she was a fantastic cook. He'd never been as physically comfortable as he was being her husband. Everything was absolutely perfect, except—

Except he desired her so very much. All the time. It never seemed to switch off, and Jack had to restrain himself—otherwise he'd have Caroline on her back, fucking her hard, more or less all the time—day and night—and that wasn't good.

The desire was sometimes like a low-level ache, sometimes as sharp as a snakebite, but there, always.

Still . . . it was early morning. They'd last made love the previous night, before midnight. Technically, it was another day, wasn't it?

And if he didn't have her right now he'd die.

There would be a point in their marriage when he'd cool off, he knew there would be—he just didn't know when.

She was wearing one of those silky nightgowns he loved. When he slid his hand under the gown, he could feel the silk of her skin along his palms and the silk of the gown against the back of his hand.

He was spooned around her, a position both of them loved. He felt her smooth warmth all along his front, and even in sleep it felt like he could protect her. Surround her with his body, arms tucked around her middle. He felt like the dragon protecting the princess. During the day he had to let her go out into the world, of course. And he couldn't be there all day by her side, armed and ready. Even he understood that. So all day as he went about his business, he had a low-level hum of worry about her. In the very beginning of their marriage he'd call a billion times a day just to hear her voice.

He'd almost lost her to a violent man from his own violent past, and the image of those last moments . . . the raging snowstorm, a soldier rising from cover with Caroline in his sights, finger tightening on the trigger . . . he shuddered at the memory and Caroline stirred.

She'd gently taught him that she was okay, that he didn't have to worry about her and he didn't have to call a hundred times a day. Violence in Summerville was rare. What were the odds of violent lightning striking twice?

Still, he insisted on giving her self-defense lessons, which she accepted and treated as gym classes. He was on a campaign to teach her firearms use but so far she'd refused with a shudder.

The imperative to keep Caroline safe while accepting that she had a life was a constant struggle.

But, by God, at night and in bed, that was when she was completely safe and all his.

His left hand cupped her thigh, relishing the silky smooth feel of her.

They liked to sleep with the curtains open. There was a full moon framed by the window, bathing the room with silvery light.

Caroline was so beautiful in daylight. Her colors came out in sunlight—the bright red-gold of her hair, that ivory skin with a faint blush underneath—but in moonlight she turned to marble perfection. Like now.

Jack watched, fascinated, as his hand slowly smoothed up her thigh, taking the silky nightgown with it. His hand was large and dark and rough, an erotic contrast to the pale smoothness of the skin of her thigh.

She was awake now, he could tell. And getting ready. The faint smell of roses drifted up. She didn't use perfume but her soap and body lotions and shampoo were all rose-scented. When she was aroused her skin heated up, and it was like having sex in a rose garden.

His hand smoothed over her hip. Caroline gave up wearing panties to bed in the first week of their marriage, honeymooning in Hawaii. Looking back on it, Jack realized he overdid it. On their honeymoon it was as if he'd never had sex in his entire life and was making up for it now that he was married.

He'd had sex, of course. Tons of it. Just not sex with Caroline, which was something so different there should be another word for it. Caro-sex, maybe.

Looking back on that first week of their honeymoon in Hawaii, his main memories were of their eating and swimming and of his cock in her.

One night they'd fallen asleep together while he was still erect and inside her. He'd been wiped out from nonstop lovemaking. He'd just gone out like a light inside her and woke himself up when his body took over in the morning and started moving.

Now Caroline sighed when his hand smoothed over her belly, shifting her hips closer to his. The hairs on the back of his neck stood up. He put his lips to the soft skin behind her ear and breathed in, trying not to sniff her like a dog. God, she always smelled so wonderful. And her arousal—ah, yes.

His hand drifted down, cupped her. She was warm and soft and starting to get excited. Jack had a keen sense of smell and could tell what stage she'd reached by smell alone sometimes.

She was starting to get ready and he was already at the starting gate, frantically revving the pedal.

Ah well, getting her to where he could enter her was always a pleasure. *Concentrate on that*, he told himself, ignoring his swollen dick.

Another small sigh as he outlined the lips of her sex with his fingers. "Good morning," he whispered in her ear, then bit her earlobe lightly.

She shuddered, her entire body moving against him. "It's not morning," she whispered. Her eyes opened, looked outside the window where the full moon was disappearing under the sill. "It's still night."

"Well, I'm feeling really, really awake," Jack said, and pressed himself against her backside.

Her smile was in her voice. "Yes, love. I can tell."

She lifted so he could pull her nightgown up and off, flinging it high so he could watch it billow down like a parachute made of pale pink silk. He didn't want her to wear panties because it was a barrier, but that moment in which he took off her nightgown and watched it float in the air—man. Pure sex.

"We won't need that," he growled in her ear, lifting her thigh with his.

"No, we won't need it," she whispered, taking in a deep breath. He could see her narrow rib cage rise and fall, breasts free for his hands. This was when he wished he had four of them. One to slide along her thighs, one to enter her, one to caress her breasts, one to let her soft hair run through his fingers.

Sex with Caroline was such a feast, a riot of colors and tastes and textures and scents. Each one delightful, each something to linger over if he didn't have the drum beat of fierce desire spurring him on.

Like now.

He wanted to rush things, wanted to get in her fast. Luckily, he knew some short cuts. This past year he'd studied Caroline like a medical student studies physiology. He knew her down to the bone.

For instance, he knew she went crazy when he kissed her neck. Caroline's neck was Pleasure Central, right after the soft, sensitive region between her thighs. But the neck was a close second.

His lips ran softly along a tendon, up and down that long, slender neck. By the second run, her sighs were starting to sound like moans. He bit her lightly, then licked her skin. She jumped and her body seemed to pulse with heat. The smell of roses intensified. He closed his eyes as he kissed her neck so he could concentrate on her soft skin and the smell of roses mixed with the scent of her arousal, a combination he was addicted to.

God, how had he not understood how much he'd been missing before? Maybe because all of this was possible only with Caroline. She was the missing link.

Soft, biting kisses as he pulled her closer, nudging the head of his cock against her softness. God, that felt good—so good he moaned in her ear and felt her contract around him, soft and wet now.

"Put me in you," he whispered in her ear, so close his breath must have been like a caress because she shivered.

"Okay," she whispered back.

Oh yeah.

Jack slid his hand up to cover her belly, right over where a child of theirs would grow . . .

Caroline was holding him while opening herself up and she jerked a little as she felt him suddenly swell even larger. "Wow. Whatever that thought was, hold it."

"You bet." Oh yeah. Caroline, growing larger and larger every day. They'd hear the baby's heart beat at one point; she'd feel it move inside her.

Jack hoped with all his heart that they'd have a little girl who looked just like Caroline. Whatever they had, their

child—or, even better, children—would for each of them be
their only blood relation in this world.

He lifted her leg higher and she was completely exposed.
Looking down over her shoulder, he could see two small, pale,
perfect breasts; a tiny waist; flat belly; and—whoa—paradise. Puffy pink lips peeping out through ash-brown hair, her
pretty hands holding him and holding herself open.

Clutching her tightly, he moved his hips forward, feeling
her welcome every inch of the way. Her entire body opened to
him. Her cunt, her legs, an arm reaching back. He loved this
moment, when his body entered hers, when they were one,
when he was home.

He always stopped at this moment simply to savor it.
Inside the love of his life, part of her, whole at last.

But then, of course, his body took over. He was a guy and
this was the moment when rosy, fuzzy thoughts of together-
ness fled his head and all he could think about was how warm
she was, how tight she was . . . it blew his mind. His brain just
. . . left. And he was merely the sum total of his senses, unable
to think—just feel.

When he came, Jack gave a great shout muffled in her
hair. He retained just enough consciousness to fall asleep by
her side and not on top of her while the rich blackness took
him away.

He must have slept for a couple of hours. When he opened
his eyes again the sky outside the window was pearly white,
the sun behind the clouds shedding a diffuse light. The fore-
cast was for snow late in the afternoon.

His eyes had popped open and he lay grinning in bed for a

moment. He felt *great*. Like he could conquer the world while running a marathon and playing the piano at the same time. His body twitched and danced with energy. He lifted his head to see Caroline's face, hoping she was awake or at least close to waking.

Nope. Out like a light.

He slid out of bed and stretched tall, King of the Mountain, then dropped for a fast fifty push-ups. Which was nothing, considering in the Rangers they'd done a hundred and fifty before breakfast and another hundred before lunch. He knew he'd give himself a good workout at his gym today; this was just to get the blood moving. Not that he needed it—his blood was flowing just fine.

A quick shower and he was by the bedside, watching Caroline sleep.

He clapped his hands, which usually worked to wake her instantly. This time she didn't even open her eyes, just flapped one hand as she snuggled deeper into the pillow.

"Go away," she mumbled.

Nope.

Jack shook her shoulder gently. "We have to train. There are a few new moves I want to show you, honey."

When he'd almost lost her to violence a year ago, he'd vowed to teach her self-defense, and he had. She didn't take the lessons too seriously but by sheer dint of repetition, she had some moves in her. He wanted to deepen that knowledge, drill it into her muscle memory so that when she needed it, if she was ever in trouble, it would come automatically.

As a soldier, Jack had trained endlessly and it had saved his life countless times. Sweat in training saves blood in battle. That had been drummed into him incessantly, and it was true.

Trouble could come from anywhere, at any time. Caroline had been born wealthy into a loving family, so her formative years had been spent far from trouble. Jack had been born into trouble. His entire life had been spent at risk and he reacted accordingly.

If this were a kind world, a just world, trouble would never find Caroline again. She'd had her fill, paid her dues—that side of the slate was in balance. But of course, life wasn't like that. Violence and danger were everywhere and didn't discriminate.

Twice Caroline had been in danger and had had no tools at all in her head or in her body to help herself. All the beauty and kindness and smarts in the world don't help when you're dealing with scum, and the world was full of scumbags.

It drove Jack a little crazy to think of trouble finding Caroline again. Because much as he tried to protect her—their home had been so revamped from a security point of view it could have been featured in *Beautiful Secure Homes & Fortress Gardens*—he couldn't be there 24/7. So the only way he could keep sane was to try to drill her in self-defense.

He was a little OCD about it, that was true. And Caroline wasn't too motivated. That was true, too. But it was the only thing he absolutely insisted on in their marriage. Everything else was her call. The house was decorated the way she wanted it, and they ate what she cooked, they travelled where she wanted to go, they saw the movies she wanted to see. Jack was fine with it all, as long as he was indulged in this.

"Come on, honey," he said when she didn't move.

"It's Christmas Eve, Jack." There was a little whine in there, which made him grin.

"Yeah? Training stops for no man."

"How about for women?"

"For no woman, either."

As an answer she burrowed deeper into the nest of blankets.

Stalemate.

Nothing left to do but use the atom bomb.

"I'll let you throw me," Jack said slyly.

Both eyes opened, focused on him.

"Yeah?" she said, interested.

He knew enough not to smile. "Yeah."

It was fairly painful, throwing himself to the mat, but he did it for her from time to time so she could have the feel of it in her hands and muscles.

"Twice." She made it a statement.

He frowned.

"Twice. You'll let me throw you twice."

Ouch. "Okay," he said on a sigh. "Twice."

She gave a sunny smile and threw the blankets back.

First Page Bookstore
Late afternoon, Christmas Eve

"And here I have lamely related to you the uneventful chronicle of two foolish children in a flat who most unwisely sacrificed for each other the greatest treasures of their house.

But in a last word to the wise of these days, let it be said that of all who give gifts, these two were the wisest."

Caroline closed the book and smiled at her audience—twenty kids who lived in homeless shelters and foster homes in Summerville and Mona, ten miles away.

She'd deliberately chosen *The Gift of The Magi*.

An old-fashioned tale of old-fashioned feelings—love, tenderness, sacrifice.

Feelings utterly foreign to the kids gathered in front of her. Their lives were dark and dangerous. Many of them had been betrayed by the very people who were supposed to protect them.

At first, they'd squirmed as they started to understand that the story wouldn't be slam-bang fast like video games and the few TV shows they watched on ancient donated sets in the shelters. There were words they clearly didn't understand and which she carefully explained. *Pier glass, fob, meretricious*.

She skirted around O. Henry's meaning of "chorus girls," painfully aware that several of the kids had moms who gave blow jobs in back seats for twenty five bucks apiece. The language was archaic and slow and foreign to them. The emotions, too.

But they got there. Because, although the type of love that existed in the story wasn't one they'd seen firsthand, it was something every human aspired to. Something everyone instinctively understood.

They were baffled at first, looking around at each other, rolling their eyes as the story unfolded. But, as she suspected they would be, they were slowly drawn in, helplessly attracted by the kind of experiences they'd likely never encountered. Generosity and true love.

Her husband, Jack, had grown up as they had.

Worse, even. Some of these kids, like little Manuel sitting quietly at the outer edges of the group, had mothers who loved them. His stepfather was a drug addict who was so violent there was a restraining order against him. But Manuel's mother cared for Manuel. Caroline sometimes did readings in his shelter and he always nestled at her side like a small brown bird. Clothes old but carefully mended and clean.

Jack had never had a mother's love. He had never known his mother. All he'd known was shelter after shelter in the grip of a violent drunk for a father.

Utterly unlike her own early experience of life in the embrace of a solid, loving family. She'd lost her family to tragedy at twenty, but nothing could ever erase two decades of love.

Jack had turned into the finest man she knew, thanks to his rock-solid character and a few lucky breaks. These kids, too—born and raised in degradation—could turn their lives around. All they needed was to know that it was possible.

If you believed something was possible, you could make it come true. Caroline believed that from the bottom of her heart.

At the end, there was utter silence in the room, so different from the squirming and punching and shouting at the beginning. It had started to snow and in the silence you could hear the odd needle of sleet embedded in the snow as it hit the windows. Though the kids suffered in the cold, with frayed clothes and inadequate shoes, the few heads that turned to the window smiled at the snow falling like clouds, making the lit store windows along State Street glow with an unearthly light.

Caroline was glad that a sense of beauty hadn't been beaten out of them yet.

"So, kids." She put the book away carefully and leaned forward, looking each child in the eye. Unconsciously they leaned forward, too, watching her. Realizing that she *saw* them. Was listening to them.

I was invisible, her husband had said of his early life in shelters. *Nobody saw me except you.*

"What happened? How did Jim show his love for his wife?"

It had been a suggestion of her father, to volunteer at the shelter—she who had grown up with so much. Her eyes had been opened and she'd discovered an entire new layer of reality. Including befriending a tall, gangly boy who'd been hungrier for learning than he'd been for food. She'd brought him books he devoured until she realized he was also literally hungry, and started bringing sandwiches together with books.

He'd disappeared one Christmas and she hadn't seen him again until he showed up twelve years later—a man so completely changed she hadn't recognized him.

These kids felt as invisible as Jack had felt. There were more and more of them in this recession—women and children falling through the cracks. Unseen, unwanted, unloved.

Small arms were waving, like branches in the wind in a tiny forest. "Me, me, me!" they cried.

Caroline smiled. She was determined to let every kid speak, be heard. Then they would troop across the street to

Sylvie's tea shop, where hot chocolate and muffins and a gift book for every child awaited. *The Hunger Games.* Because Jim and Della were the ideal, but Katniss . . . Katniss showed that you could grow up in terrible circumstances and you could still fight back—and prevail.

"Okay, Jamal." She pointed to a kid in the front row, whose eyes had grown larger and larger as the story progressed. She knew each kid's story—she'd insisted on it. She wanted to know who they were, what their lives were about. Jamal had no father and five half-siblings, all from different men. "How did Jim show his love for Della?"

"He sold his watch so he could buy a comb for her."

Yes, indeed. She'd read *The Gift of the Magi* a million times but it still made her smile.

"That's right. And why did he have to sell the watch?"

Silence. The reason was so very close to their lives. "Because he was poor," one girl whispered finally. "They were both poor." Shawna, who was twelve but so thin she looked eight.

"He could have stolen the comb and kept his watch," Caroline gently suggested. Twenty small heads nodded. Yes indeed, he could have. "Why didn't he?"

Silence once more. Why Jim hadn't stolen the comb was not very clear to them. In their world, a lot of people stole. It was just a question of not getting caught.

"Because . . ." a shy voice said, a slight lisp on the *s*. He couldn't be seen because he was behind Mack, who was huge for his age, but Caroline knew who it was. Manuel. Manuel, whose mother had been put in the hospital five times in the past year by his stepfather and was in the hospital right now.

"Because?" Caroline said.

"Because it showed how much he loved her."

"That's right, Manuel. Not stealing the comb—but rather, sacrificing something he cared about to buy something for her—showed how much he loved his wife. And she made a sacrifice too, didn't she? Who can tell me what she sacrificed?" Another forest of small arms. "Lucy?"

"Her hair. She sold her hair for him," Lucy sighed. Her mother was an addict who sold herself to buy drugs. Lucy'd been a ward of the state several times while her mother went to rehab. True love wasn't a big part of her world.

"That's right. So, kids, if you could buy anything at all for your mom or your dad or a sister or brother—what would it be?"

"Anything at all?" Jamal asked, scrunching his face up in puzzlement.

"Go wild," Caroline smiled. "Anything at all."

"PlayStation 4, for my mom," Jamal said decisively, and the room erupted in laughter.

It was an interesting exercise. It was probably the first time they'd ever thought about being able to get anything themselves without stealing it. And, for many, the first time they'd thought of sharing. Their lives were impoverished in every way there was. The gift ideas were all over the place—a house, a job, a dad out of prison, a trip to Disneyland, a pair of red shoes, a new car. Everyone spoke but Manuel.

Caroline watched him, sitting small and quiet. Trying very hard not to be noticed.

Jack had told her about his early childhood, when he'd been small and weak. Perfecting the art of sliding by without attracting attention because attention was, more often than not, painful. Hiding in the shadows, never speaking, because anything could set his father off. And even when not speaking, his father could fill himself with rage all by himself.

Then Jack had grown big and strong and no one bothered him after the age of fourteen.

But before then, before filling out, he'd been prey. He'd taken care of that by joining the army and then the super elite soldiers, the Rangers. Jack was definitely not prey any more. And Jack had made it his life's work to teach the weak to defend themselves.

He was a security consultant, a very successful one. If you were a bank or a corporation and you wanted his expert help, he was happy to give it, at a premium price. He also ran a dojo school and fitness center, and if you were a lawyer or an executive hoping to firm up your abs and glutes, why, Jack was your man—at two hundred dollars an hour, when you could get him.

But if you were young and poor—and above all, if you were female—you got the best help in the world and the bill was torn up.

While the kids proposed wild presents, she glanced out the window at the Cup of Tea. Across the street her friend Sylvie waved. A big table with a red tablecloth, plastic cups and a huge thermos, and festive red plates had been set out in the center of the tea shop. Along the counter were enough muffins to feed a brigade of soldiers—just waiting for the kids. Time to wrap this up.

One more kid.

"Manuel? What do you think your mom would like as a present?"

He was silent a long moment, long enough for the chattering of the kids to die down. He swallowed, small Adam's apple bobbing. "For my step-dad to die," he whispered.

Caroline actually felt her heart contract—with pity, with sorrow, with the heaviness of painful truth. Because it *was* true. Manuel's life and his mother's life would be infinitely better without that violent monster in it.

It wasn't until she'd worked in the shelter that she'd even known there was such a thing as bad fathers in the world. Her own father had been wonderful—loving and generous and fun. A larger-than-life figure whose love for his wife and children was manifested a thousand times a day.

Caroline was pregnant. She'd taken the test first thing this morning in the bookshop. She knew how much Jack wanted a child, so she didn't run the test at home. No sense disappointing him. Somehow, though, even before the strip had turned red, she knew.

Just as she knew, beyond a shadow of a doubt, that Jack would be a marvelous father. He'd probably be wildly over-protective, as he was with her, but he'd be there for his children in every way there was. She also had no doubt that he'd give his life for her without question. As he would for any children they might have.

Jack had come late to love, but he cherished it. Caroline hoped with all her heart that the young souls in front of her would one day experience the precious gift of love for themselves.

She thought of all she had in her own life—a loving husband, the beautiful home she'd grown up in, the prospect of a child to love—with enormous gratitude, because between the death of her family when she was twenty and the sudden, mysterious reappearance of Jack in her life, there had been hard, barren years. Years in which she'd cared for a sick brother, had watched her friends disappear one by one as her life grew harder and money grew scarcer. Years of working hard and watching her brother die, inch by slow inch. Years in which she couldn't allow herself to cry at night because Toby would have noticed her swollen eyes and blamed himself. Years of hardship and sorrow.

She knew firsthand how hard it was to hope when all around you is bleakness and despair.

But on this Christmas Eve, at least there'd be hot chocolate and muffins and a book for these children.

She clapped her hands. "Kids! Let's get ready! Put on your coats because we're going across the street for a treat."

The artificial lull created by the storytelling was over. The noise level rose and the twenty kids seemed to become a hundred and fifty as they pulled on ragged coats and dirty scarves.

The noise level was so loud she didn't hear the bell over the shop door ring, and only understood that someone had entered because within a minute, all the kids fell silent.

She looked behind her and froze.

Oh shit, was her first thought. She was instantly ashamed of it. The man who entered looked like a thug, but she knew better than to judge solely on appearance. One of Jack's best friends looked like an extra out of *Resident Evil*—rode a big black bike and spoke in a low growl—and was a sweetheart.

This man had the *Resident Evil* vibe down pat, but he didn't look like a sweetheart at all.

While her head was running through all this, her body went right ahead into overdrive. Sweat broke out all over and her heart kicked into a thumping beat guaranteed to pulse blood to her extremities simply because her body recognized that she was going to need it.

Nonetheless, ten thousand years of civilization and her mother's strict upbringing had her asking in a perfectly normal tone, "May I help you?"

The man had been scanning the room but at her voice he turned slowly toward her, and her involuntary danger signals started booming.

He was truly huge—taller even than Jack, and seemingly twice as broad. But where Jack was all tight muscle, this man looked like vats of lard had been thrown onto his frame before he'd been shoehorned into clothes. Underneath the fat, though, there had once been muscle. He must have weighed three hundred pounds, every ounce mean and stinking.

The stench reached across the room. Booze, unwashed clothes, unwashed man, and that awful something some humans emanated that was like a dog whistle to normal people. *This man is crazy.* She'd seldom come across it, but it was unmistakable.

There was absolute silence. The kids all had an instinctive understanding that danger had just walked into the room. They'd lived shoulder to shoulder with danger. Several of the kids were hunched in on themselves as if to make themselves smaller. Some had hidden under her desk, in corners; some stood frozen, white-faced.

The man was dressed in filthy leather pants and a leather vest with no shirt, as if impervious to the cold outside. He shook the snow off himself like a polar bear and took a step forward.

God, he was *big*.

Jack had taught Caroline a lot of martial arts moves but there was nothing she could do against someone this massive. She simply didn't have the weight or muscle mass.

And anyway, the guy was flying higher than a kite.

Looking closer, it was clear. The pupils were dilated and his eyes were slightly unfocused. He swayed a little where he stood as if he were in a strong wind, though there was no wind in her bookstore. Just twenty little kids and a very frightened bookshop owner.

"Can I help you?" she repeated, keeping her voice neutral and soft, exactly as if she were trying to calm a wild beast.

"Help me?" he repeated. "Can you fucking help me? Yeah, lady. Yeah, you can help me." His eyes narrowed. "Looking for my boy. Manuel."

Oh God, oh God. This man didn't only look dangerous, he *was* dangerous. He'd nearly killed his wife. He was like a walking bomb in her bookshop—a bookshop filled with twenty young kids. Her breath clogged in her lungs. She didn't dare look around, but from what she could see in her peripheral vision, Manuel had disappeared.

"So." The man swayed. For a second she hoped that he'd simply collapse to the ground, stoned, but he stayed on his feet. "Where the fuck's my boy?"

Caroline swallowed heavily. She heard Jack's voice in her head. *What do you do if you sense trouble, honey?*

They'd gone over it a million times, and each and every time they talked about it, he tried to convince her to carry a weapon. He'd lived in a dangerous world all his life and he was always armed in some way.

Not to mention the fact that, to a certain extent, Jack's entire body was a weapon.

"Where is he?" the man bellowed, voice hoarse and cracking. "Where the fuck is my boy? Where's that little shit?" Her heart nearly stopped when he reached behind him and a big black knife appeared in his hand.

In that instant, Caroline regretted bitterly not taking Jack up on his constant offers to teach her how to shoot. Oh man, if she had a gun and knew how to use it, she'd drill him right between the eyes—without any compunction at all, because it was clear he was here to hurt.

His black, piggy eyes scanned the room with a narrow focus and he moved toward the kids. One girl screamed, the sound abruptly cut off by her own hand. The kids were like small animals, hoping to avoid the gaze of the predator in their midst.

The man growled at the girl, moving forward unsteadily.

Caroline stepped in front of him. He swatted her away backhanded like a bothersome fly.

His blow took her by surprise. She landed against the corner of the bookshelf, the breath knocked out of her, and nearly passed out from the pain. She hung onto consciousness ferociously, understanding that she was the only thing between those kids and tragedy.

"Manuel!" the crazy guy screamed, the booming voice echoing in the room. He brandished the knife. "Come out, you little shithead! You're a worm, just like your fucking mom! Don't have the courage to come out, eh? Then I'm coming after you!"

He lurched forward and Caroline watched, horrified, as he plowed into the kids. Those who weren't quick enough to scramble out of the way were swatted away, as she had been.

She'd nearly been knocked unconscious by those huge ham hands. He could do real damage to a thin eight-year-old.

Though her head was still spinning, she rolled to her knees, waited for some strength in her limbs. The kids were crying, screaming, two lying in little heaps on the ground.

Caroline gritted her teeth and rose unsteadily to her feet. As she rose, she glanced across the street and saw Sylvie staring, wide-eyed. The man's back was to her so Caroline pantomimed a phone to her ear. Sylvia grabbed a cell from the counter and punched three numbers in.

9-1-1. Good girl.

Sylvie spoke into the phone, clearly reporting what was happening in First Page. A huge man armed with a knife, a roomful of kids, and a potential hostage situation. They'd want to know numbers and positions and Sylvie spoke for a full minute.

Sylvie gave a thumbs up and Caroline motioned for her to get down, since she was highlighted in the huge picture window. Sylvie dropped from sight.

"Come out, you little fucker!" the monster was screaming. Except for the two small heaps, all the kids had scrambled out of his way. He didn't pay them any attention, focusing on his specific prey.

Please, Manuel, run out the back door, she prayed. Maybe he had, because he was nowhere to be found. Monster Man was roaring with rage, upending bookcases, scattering books and magazines, shattering a lamp.

Caroline's mind cleared. The first thing to do was get as many kids out of here as possible. While the monster was bellowing, wallowing in his rage, she quietly went behind a waist-high counter and opened the back door. Holding a finger to her lips, she ushered out ten of the kids while the man's back was turned. When he turned around, all he saw was Caroline, who'd moved ten feet from the door. The counter hid the kids slipping out, one by one.

Now for help.

Sylvie had called for official help, but Caroline had a husband who was way more dangerous than Monster Man. She had on a sweater and a long wool jacket over it. Out of habit, she always kept her cell on her at all times. Jack had insisted early in their marriage and it was second nature by now.

Jack's cell number was the first on speed dial. "Honey, hi." His deep voice was unmistakable.

Oh God, she'd forgotten to take it off speaker!

She pressed the button to disengage speakerphone and took a chance, knocking over an earthenware bowl of apples to catch the monster's attention. He turned his head briefly. It was almost painful to watch his reflexes. He was so drugged up they were slow, stimuli penetrating with difficulty.

"Put down that knife!" she screamed, knowing Jack was listening. "There are kids here in the bookstore!"

That would be enough.

Wherever he was, Jack was coming for her now. She knew that like she knew the sun rose in the East. Monster Man paused in trashing her store to look back at her, narrow-eyed. He looked her up and down and, horribly, licked his lips, opening his mouth in a grotesque smile. His teeth were ground down and brown. "Pretty lady," he growled, and pointed the knife at her. "You're next. After the brat." Then he turned back around, looking for Manuel.

Caroline beckoned, and the kids who had been trapped behind Monster Man ran to her. She herded them behind her, pointing to the back door. Five kids were left.Jamal was by her side, trembling with fear. "Where's Manuel?" she whispered. "Did he get out?"

Jamal shook his head. "He's holed up in your office," he whispered .Oh God. The door to her office could be locked from the inside, but it was only a pine door. Monster Man could shove it in with one kick from his boots.

The five kids left were crouching behind the counter. There were none left in the shop. She had to hope that screaming Monster Man, who seemed to have the intelligence of a slug, had the attention span of one, too.

Quietly, Caroline signaled to the kids around her to scuttle to the back door. She shepherded them out as fast as she could while the man bellowed and crashed into chairs and shelves, screaming for Manuel.

Across the street, Sylvie's head peeped up over the counter and she made the OK sign, then the gun sign. Caroline nodded, then signaled for her to duck back down.

Okay. The police were here, hopefully with SWAT snipers.

She jolted at the sound of wood crashing, but what terrified her even more than that were the animal sounds Monster Man was making as he dragged little Manuel out by the hair.

High-pitched, unholy screams of rage that raised the hairs on the back of her neck and along her forearms.

To her dying day, Caroline would never forget those bestial sounds coming out of a human being's mouth. It was terrifying, like being in the room with a wild animal.

Heart in her mouth, she watched as he dragged little Manuel out by the hair to the middle of the room, stood him up, and held the knife to his throat.

What horrified her most was that the little boy didn't make a sound. White-faced and trembling, he stood as still as a soldier—even when that meaty fist pulled his hair so hard the scalp raised a little.

And Caroline knew with a sudden swift certainty that this was not the first time this had happened to Manuel. Not the first time he was terrorized and tormented by this human beast.

But by God it would be the last.

A deep calmness settled in her. That child was not leaving these premises with that monster. She'd die first.

"Where's that worthless bitch?" Manuel's stepfather screamed. He was purple-faced, sweat streaming from his temples, dripping off his cheeks. The animal smell intensified, a sickening stench. "Where's your fucking mom?"

Little Manuel's eyes were closed and his lips were moving. He was praying.

"Huh?" The man shook his stepson like a rag doll. "Where the fuck is she?"

"In the hospital," Manuel whispered.

"You fucking *liar!* You lie, just like she lies. There's nothing wrong with the bitch! All she does is lie about me!" He whipped that big black knife back up, held it to Manuel's slender throat.

Jack had put her through drills in her training. One of the drills had been observation. He'd suddenly ask her in a restaurant how many waiters there were in a room. How many lamps in a hotel room. Where the back exit was in a coffee shop. How many chairs in the bank lobby.

For a period he drilled her so hard she started observing and memorizing in exasperation, even when he wasn't there, because he was there in her head.

And now it paid off, because out of the corner of her eye she saw a slender black rod slide over the counter across the street at Sylvie's. A rifle barrel! And another rod slid over the balustrade of the rooftop of Sylvie's building. Another sniper.

The cavalry had truly arrived.

She'd learned enough of shooting from Jack to know that the expert marksmen that were behind those rifles wouldn't miss across twenty yards of street. They couldn't shoot what they couldn't see, though, and the monster was in the short side of her L-shaped shop, hidden by a wall. They could hear his bellows but they couldn't see him.

She could wait it out. Sooner or later, the snipers would get him. But if it was later, he could harm Manuel. Kill him with a flick of that meaty wrist.

Already he was working himself up into a greater state of rage, spittle at the edges of his mouth. He jerked in his agitation and a thin line of red appeared on Manuel's neck, slowly starting to drip blood.

It was terrifying to see little Manuel's calm expression. He'd seen this man beat up his mother countless times. His brown eyes lifted to the roof—to heaven—and his white lips moved more quickly.

He was preparing to die. This small, innocent child expected to die at the hands of this monster.

"Hey!" Caroline stood up, waved her hands. Across the street, through a break in the snow, she saw Sylvie's head above the counter. Sylvie's eyes opened wide in shock.

But Caroline knew what she was doing. She had a plan and it all depended on the skill and nerve of the police snipers. She trusted them. Jack was friends with more or less everyone on the force and he said they were all good guys and good cops.

They'd better be, because she was just about to put her life in their hands.

"Hey!" she yelled again. "Let that boy go, you son of a bitch!"

His eyes widened. Clearly, no one talked to him like that. At least, no woman.

There was utter silence in her bookstore while twhile Caroline walked over to the man She stopped halfway across the room. He was a bully. He used his bulk to intimidate. He'd want to come to her, loom over her. Make her scared.

If she hadn't been so incandescent with rage, maybe she would have been scared, because as he walked to her— Manuel stumbling in front of him, blood staining his beige t-shirt—she realized all over again just how huge he was. At least six-five, maybe three hundred pounds. Most of it fat, but some of it muscle. Certainly enough to hurt her. Maybe kill her.

"What do you want with M—" She almost said Manuel's

name and stopped herself just in time. If Monster Man felt she had a connection to the boy, he'd use it. "With the boy?"

"This worthless piece of trash? This fag? He snivels every time I teach him what's right and wrong. Ain't that right, boy?" He gave Manuel a vicious shake. Manuel remained utterly and completely still. Only his lips moved. *"Ain't that right, boy?"*

Sweat broke out all over her body when he pulled Manuel's head back more forcefully, exposing the throat like a lamb's at slaughter time.

"Little fucker's gonna make her come back to me. She left me. My wife fucking *left me!* Police told me I can't go near her or the boy. Well, how about this? I've got the boy and now I'll get her."

They were fully in the center of the room now, lit up like actors on a stage. Everyone outside could see exactly what the situation was. She understood completely that they didn't dare take a shot because the man was so huge he could fall on Manuel, or slit the boy's throat as he dropped.

He was also close enough to Caroline to take another swipe at her.

It was too dangerous to take a shot now. They would be watching carefully through their scopes. If matters precipitated, if he pressed the knife more closely, they just might take the shot. And it might kill Manuel.

Caroline made sure she was off to the side, affording the snipers a clear shot. "Do you want me to call her?" she asked.

"Huh?"

He frowned, the words slowly making their way through the rot and pus in his drug-addled head.

She pulled her smart-phone from her pocket, finger hovering over the screen. "Do you want me to call your wife? Tell her to come?"

Unseen by the monster, Manuel went even whiter, trying to shake his head no, though his head was held in an iron grip.

The idea had made its way through what passed for the man's brains. A wide smile broke through. "Yeah. Fuck yeah. Tell that bitch to get here pronto. I have things to say to her."

"Where is she?"

"Hospital," he said sullenly. "Faking it."

There was only one hospital in town. Caroline nodded. "I happen to have the hospital right on speed dial," she lied. "So . . . what's her name?"

"*Bitch!*" he screamed. "Her name is Bitch! Because she is one!"

"I'm sure she is," Caroline said smoothly. "But I still need a name."

"Anna." The word was dragged out of him in a snarl. "Anna Ramirez Pedersen. Sometimes she drops my name, the cunt. Just calls herself Ramirez."

"Okay. I'm calling now." She pretended to punch in a number and brought the phone to her ear. "Yes," she said brightly, as if to an receptionist. "This is Caroline Prescott at First Page. I'd like to speak with Anna Ramirez Pedersen, please."

"Honey." Jack's voice came on, deep and low. "I'm right outside. We've got rifles on the guy. The instant you and the boy drop to the floor they'll take the shot."

Oh God. Her knees nearly buckled with relief at hearing Jack's voice, a lifeline to sanity.

"Okay, yes," she answered, as if in response to someone at the hospital. "I understand. I'll wait."

"Try to get away from the window, there'll be glass everywhere," Jack said.

"Uh huh." She looked over at Monster Man. "Yes, I'll hold."

Jack was in her head now. All the thousands of hours of lessons she'd absorbed.

Combat time is in slow motion. Everything slows, including your heart rate. Don't get tunnel vision. Keep all your senses open. Observe before acting.

And damned if time didn't slow down. She took in everything—the man's stance, the angle at which he held the knife to Manuel's throat, their distance to the window.

She started hyperventilating, dragging in oxygen, and in her head calculated the three elements forming a triangle—herself, the monster holding Manuel, and the snipers outside.

She ran through her head the things that had to happen to free the little boy from his lunatic stepfather—visualized it—and acted.

Caroline had never been particularly athletic in her childhood but she had loved softball and had been an excellent pitcher.

"Yes," she said, straightening suddenly as if a new voice were on the line. "Mrs. Pedersen? Yes, there's someone who wants to talk to you."

Monster Man's eyes gleamed. Finally. The woman he was hard-wired to torment. On the phone, and with their son under threat, so she'd be guaranteed to obey and to suffer.

He was in monster heaven. With his free hand he curled his meaty fingers upwards in the universal *gimme* gesture.

Oh, yeah.

Everything slowed down even more, her movements became calculated and precise.

She pitched the phone to the man, ensuring it fell short, so he'd have to lunge to pick it up. He loosened his hold on Manuel, the knife hand moving away. While the phone was still in the air, Caroline launched herself at Manuel, taking him to the ground and rolling with him, coming to a stop with her body covering his, shielding his little head with her arms.

The world exploded.

Glass flew in bright shiny shards almost indistinguishable from the gusts of snow blowing into the shop. She looked up in horror at the red mist in the midst of the white glass and snow, then down at the man who'd fallen like a sack of meat.

Deader'n shit, as Jack said.

Good! she thought viciously.

And then she didn't have time to think anything at all because a billion men dressed in black and wielding big black guns flooded the bookstore shouting, and a white-faced Jack had pulled her up and into an embrace so tight she couldn't breathe.

He was trembling.

Her husband, tough-as-nails Jack Prescott, was trembling, and his cheeks were wet.

"God," he groaned and gave a huge shudder. "I think I lost about fifty years off my life."

Caroline reached up to kiss him, then fought free.

Four men were crouched on their haunches around the massive corpse, holding on to their rifle barrels. Blood seeped from the back of the monster's head. Caroline looked down at him, rage and hatred in her heart, a mix of emotions she'd never had before. Didn't even know she was capable of having.

He was dead and she was glad he was dead. Maybe, just maybe, Manuel and his mother could put this behind them and make a life for themselves.

An image blossomed in her head—of tiny, trembling Manuel, holding still, frozen with terror, because he knew his stepfather was perfectly capable of slitting his throat—and she hauled off and kicked the corpse in the side as hard as she could.

Four hard male faces turned to her in surprise.

"Sorry," she gritted. "Tell the coroner he fell on something."

One guy, who looked like he ate nails for breakfast, snapped off a two-fingered salute. "Yes, ma'am."

Caroline dropped to her knees next to Manuel, who was still curled up in a little ball. Her heart squeezed tightly. He looked so slight, so vulnerable. How could anyone do this to a child?

She touched the back of his head, cupping it lightly, not knowing if he wanted to be touched at all. Abused children often couldn't bear to be touched by an adult.

"It's okay," she whispered. "It's all over."

His head whipped up and he tried to turn to look back at the corpse of his stepfather, but she gently turned his face back to hers. The sadness in his gaze wrenched her heart. He wasn't crying, though. His eyes were dry. He was a tough little soldier. "I want Mama," he whispered.

The tough-looking police officer rose and crossed to them, holding out a huge hand. Caroline rose, too, with the help of Jack's strong hand because her legs felt light. She was feeling light all over, particularly her head. It was like a helium-filled balloon that would float away if it weren't attached to her neck.

The big officer kept his hand out to Manuel, waiting patiently. "We'll take you to your mama," he said gently. "She's waiting for you." His big hand didn't move. Finally, Manuel put his tiny hand in his.

Caroline let out a pent-up breath.

The police officer's eyes met hers. For such a big bruiser, he had kind eyes. "Social services is on the way over, ma'am." He waved his free hand. "For everyone else, too. All the other kids are safe out back."

Caroline shivered. The temperature in her bookshop was the same as outside. "Can the kids wait across the street, where there's hot chocolate and muffins?" she asked. "There'd be plenty of hot chocolate and muffins for your men, too."

She shivered again. It wasn't the cold, or just the cold. It was aftershock.

"Yes, ma'am. Thank you. We'll be taking your statement—"

"Tomorrow," Jack said in a hard voice. "She'll be giving her statement tomorrow. She's been through hell and I'm taking her home. Right now."

The two men stared at each other, two alpha males with two different agendas. Caroline could almost see the waves of male will battling back and forth, and the officer broke first. He looked away, then back at Jack with a huff of breath. "Okay, Prescott. Tomorrow. I'll be expecting her no later than eleven."

"Noon," her husband responded. He gestured to her ruined bookshop. "I'm sending people in to board up the windows and clean up. We'll be spending tomorrow morning here."

The cop rolled his eyes. "Okay. Noon. The hot chocolate and those muffins better be good."

"The best," Caroline promised, then sagged against Jack, the voices around her growing distant, the room turning black.

Jack scooped up his wife and walked out with her in his arms, meeting the eyes of all the cops filling the room. He was awash in fear and anxiety and would have welcomed someone trying to stop him.

He was itching for a fight, since the motherfucker with the knife was already dead.

But no one said anything—just silently shifted and made way for him in the swirling snow coming in through the shattered picture window.

It was a miracle his heart hadn't stopped when he answered his cell, only to hear the screams of children and Caroline yelling *put down that knife!*

He'd been coming back from consulting with the Chief Financial Officer of a bank about banking security. Every hair on his head had stood on end and sweat had broken out all over his body. He'd been in battle countless times, survived dozens of firefights and kept his cool. Right then, though, his entire system had gone haywire.

He was perfectly equipped, by nature and by training, to deal with threats to himself. He had no defenses against threats to Caroline—none. There was nothing in his system that could handle this.

It had begun to snow, but he'd gunned the engine, running through red lights, taking corners so tightly he'd have tipped over if he hadn't been a combat driving instructor.

Smart Caroline. She'd managed to alert him to the threat and to where she was. He'd made a beeline to the bookstore while listening to what was happening inside First Page. He'd parked half a block away and pulled out the loaded Glock he kept in a concealed holder under the driver's seat, leaping out of the Explorer before it stopped rocking on its chassis.

He was tackled before he'd taken ten steps, and did some serious damage before he realized he was fighting a SWAT officer.

Even then, the drumbeat of Caroline in danger pounded in his head.

"Sitrep!" he'd barked at the first face he recognized. Sgt. Glenn Baker. Good guy with a gun, good guy to have on your side, good guy all around. Except right now he was keeping him from Caroline.

"Arne Pedersen, thirty-four, rap sheet as long as my dick. Likes beating up on his wife, Anna, who is currently in the county hospital. There's a restraining order against him—which he has just broken—so with that and endangerment, he's going away for a long time, no matter what. He's holding his stepson hostage. Wants his wife. Who is still in a coma. Our medic says he's hopped up. Here, get a look."

Baker put a restraining hand on Jack's shoulder, then showed him a video feed off his cell, and Jack froze. Huge guy, holding a Ka-Bar to a little boy's throat. The knife was already biting into the skin, blood seeping from a cut.

It would take nothing for the bruiser to slice the boy open.

And there was Caroline, several feet off. White-faced, staring at the man in anger.

"Here." Jack handed over his cell to Baker. "It's an open line."

They put the two feeds together—video and audio—and followed what was happening. Baker was talking quietly to his team through his boom mic.

He suddenly heard Caroline's voice clearly, talking into the cell. "This is Caroline Prescott at First Page. I'd like to speak with Anna Ramirez Pedersen, please."

"Honey," Jack said in a low voice, meeting Baker's eyes. "I'm right outside. We've got rifles on the guy. The instant you and the boy get down, they'll take the shot."

Baker notified the team and Jack stood away from the line of sight, heart pounding, listening to Caroline orchestrate the takedown. Admiring her courage, wishing for his sake she was more of a wimp, understanding very well that she was saving that little boy's life.

At risk to her own.

But now he was holding her. At the thought he might have lost her, he shuddered again.

A warm hand against his face. "Jack." Caroline smiled at him. "Don't look like that. I'm fine."

"I'm not," he answered, shifting her in his arms so he could open the passenger-side door.

They'd reached his SUV, the driver-side door still open, snow collecting in the footwell.

He placed her in the passenger seat—which was dry, thank God—and rounded the vehicle. Once she was belted in with a blanket from the back over her, he took off, trying to make it home as fast as he could before his nerves gave out.

"Well," Caroline said, picking at the blanket, looking at him out of the corner of her eye. "That was interesting."

He ground his teeth so hard the sound was audible.

"What's the matter, Jack?" She placed her pretty hand on his forearm, as she'd done a thousand times before. She often touched him while talking to him—as if judging his reactions through his skin—and he loved it.

He loved everything she did. He loved everything she said. He loved her.

"I almost lost you," he said through gritted teeth.

Caroline sighed. "Yes, but you didn't. 'Almost' only counts in horseshoes."

"And hand grenades," he answered without thinking, watching her.

"What?"

"The whole quote is '"Almost" only counts in horseshoes and hand grenades.'"

"Oh. Makes sense." She reached out to turn his face back to the road. "Pay attention. Just because I tricked death once today doesn't mean we can't still die."

She was right, damn it. He kept his face turned to the

road, though all his attention was on the pale, fragile woman by his side.

"I thought I was going to lose you," Jack said, his voice tight. "I don't think I could live without you."

"You're not going to have to." Her voice was gentle and soothing, as if he'd been in danger and not she. Except she seemed to be calm and he was all over the place. Skin too tight, nerves twitching, heart racing.

Mr. Cool, losing it.

He'd almost lost her. The thought was there, like a burr biting into his skin—making him sweat, making him bleed. He'd almost lost her.

Jack couldn't even contemplate living his life without Caroline by his side. This past year had been the happiest of his life. Going back to the bleak emptiness of Before Caroline was unthinkable. He couldn't do it, simply couldn't.

His hands were slick on the steering wheel by the time he drove into the garage.

Something was happening to him, something big. He felt like he was about to explode if he didn't do something, something . . . right . . . *now*.

But what?

The answer came when he gave Caroline his hand to help her out of the vehicle, and her skin burned against his.

What to do?

Fuck her.

Get in her and stay in her as long as was possible, because while he was in her nothing bad could ever happen to her. He could keep her safe, keep her his. Nothing else would do.

He was as hard as a rock, every nerve ending sparking like torn electric wires.

"Jack?" Caroline's voice rose, startled, as he headed through the house with her in tow. Nearly running up the stairs, striding fast down the hallway to their bedroom, where he slammed the door behind them with his boot and stood in the middle of the room, breathing hard, holding both her hands in his. "Jack, darling. What's wrong?"

Caroline kept her voice low and soothing as if he were a wild animal—and that's exactly how he felt. He was sure his eyes showed the whites all around like a panicked pony.

Jack looked at her, at his miracle of a wife. Grace, goodness, and beauty. A woman in a million, and he'd nearly lost her.

He told her his deepest truth. "I need you," he whispered hoarsely. "Right now. If I don't have you right now, I think I'll die."

She stepped closer to him, closer still, until her breasts touched his jacket, watching his eyes all the time. "My darling Jack." She lifted herself up on tiptoe and awkwardly kissed the side of his mouth. "I'm yours. You know that."

His control broke. His hands fisted in her hair and he kissed her hard, almost savagely. He knew he was bruising her mouth but he couldn't stop himself. It was as if her mouth were giving him life. He would stay alive as long as he was kissing her.

He picked her up and carried her to the bed, landing on top of her, still kissing her. Somehow he got them both naked, ripping her underwear, but it didn't matter because then he was touching her silky-soft skin all over—particularly the silky-soft *wet* skin between her legs—and it blew all his circuits.

He couldn't wait—not one second more—and entered her with one long hard thrust. He was so careful with her, always, but this time he couldn't be careful, couldn't be gentle; he needed to possess her the way he needed to breathe.

He pumped in her—hard, fast thrusts that made the headboard beat against the wall—and watched her face move up and down under him, breasts swaying to his beat. Her head was arched back, eyes closed, breathing heavy. Her arms and legs were wrapped around him, holding him tightly. She, too, was celebrating the escape from danger with sex.

Jack groaned, cupping her buttocks, moving his hands down to her thighs, lifting the backs of them higher. The fit became deeper, tighter.

He fucked her with the full strength of his body, mindless heat filling his head. He couldn't slow down, couldn't do anything but ride her as hard and as fast as he was able.

Caroline groaned and she tightened around him, one strong pulse. It lit him up and he moved even faster and harder, in an almost brutal rhythm that would shame him later but which now seemed as inevitable as the tides. Simply the way it had to be.

Another sharp pulse and another. Caroline cried out and he swelled inside her and then exploded, his entire body electrified by something that was more than sex, more than an orgasm.

This was something he'd never felt before, as if the universe itself were moving through him. He moved his face to the pillow and shouted into it as he came and came endlessly in the strongest orgasm he'd ever had.

When it was over, he realized he was plastered to his love with his own sweat. He was panting, completely drained. He turned his head to see if she was all right, but he never completed the move because he fell into a sleep so deep it could have been a coma.

Christmas Day

"Get up, sleepyhead! We've got some training to do. Today you're going to start teaching me how to shoot. I want to be Annie Oakley!"

The words came from several universes away and barely made sense to him.

Someone shook his shoulder.

Jack didn't even have the strength to open his eyes. He was under some kind of boulder that wouldn't let him move his muscles.

"Jack, wake up!"

A finger pulled up one eyelid and he saw a sideways Caroline, watching him with bright eyes.

How could she be bright-eyed when he felt like he'd been hit by a train?

"Open both those baby browns," she crooned. "That's right. Good boy."

He could open his eyes, barely, but nothing else could move. He was utterly and completely wiped out.

His eyes tracked around the room. It was morning, the

pale pearly light of a snowy morning filtering in through the windows. How could it be morning when two seconds ago he'd fallen asleep?

"Get up, get up! We've got work to do!" his wife cried. "Training, cleaning up the bookstore, celebrating Christmas . . . and celebrating something even more important. But first—Rambette!"

She was grinning. He blinked. Her eyes were bright and her color was high. She was dressed for the outdoors, mittens hanging from her parka by their strings. She danced in place like a boxer.

Jack licked dry lips. "Work?" he croaked. How could she have all this energy when he felt like he'd died a week ago?

"I'm going to start training seriously, and by God, you were right!"

Jack blinked, his thought processes fuzzy and slow. "I was?"

"Absolutely! I need to train harder and I need to know how to shoot. And I'm going to *pack heat!* I'm going to get myself a pink shoulder holster and no one is ever going to mess with me again. Ever!"

He smiled. She was so amazingly beautiful right now. "Yeah?"

"Yup." She nodded sharply. "And today—I'm going to throw you. For real."

And she did.

If you enjoyed
RECKLESS NIGHT
and
HOT SECRETS,
read on to see where the stories began in
Lisa Marie Rice's Dangerous series

Dangerous Lover

Dangerous Secrets

Dangerous Passion

Available Now

Dangerous Lover

Summerville, Washington
St. Jude Homeless Shelter
Christmas Eve

He needed Caroline like he needed light and air. More.

The tall, emaciated boy dressed in rags rose from his father's lifeless body sprawled bonelessly on the icy, concrete floor of the shelter.

His father had been dying for a long time—most of his life, in fact. There had always been something in him that didn't want to live. The boy couldn't remember the last time he'd seen his father clean and sober. He had no mother. All his life, it had been just the two of them, father and son, drifting from shelter to shelter, staying until they were kicked out.

The boy stood for a moment, looking down at his only blood relation in this world, dead in a pool of vomit and shit. Nobody had noticed his father's dead body yet. Nobody ever noticed them or even looked their way if they could help it. Even the other lost, hopeless souls in the shelter recognized someone worse off than they were and shunned them.

The boy looked around at the averted faces, eyes cast to the floor.

Nobody cared that the drunk wasn't getting up again. Nobody cared what happened to his son.

There was nothing for the boy here. Nothing.

He had to get to Caroline.

He had to move fast before they discovered that his father was dead. If they found the body here, the police and social workers and administrators would come for him. He was eighteen, but he couldn't prove it. And he knew enough about the way things worked to know that he'd become a ward of the state. He'd be locked up in some prisonlike orphanage.

No. No way. He'd rather die.

The boy moved toward the stairs that would take him up out of the shelter into the gelid, sleety afternoon.

An old woman looked up as he passed by, cloudy eyes flickering with recognition. Susie. Ancient, toothless Susie. She wasn't lost in alcohol like his father. She was lost in the smoky depths of her own mind.

"Ben, chocolate chocolate?" she cackled and smacked her wrinkled, rubbery lips. He'd once shared a chocolate bar Caroline had brought him, and Susie had looked to him for sweets ever since.

Here he was known as Ben. In the last shelter—Portland,

was it?—his father had called him Dick. Naming him after the manager of the shelter always bought them some time. Not enough. Eventually, the shelters got sick of his father's drunken rages and found a way to kick them out.

Susie's hands, with their long, black, ragged nails, grasped at him. Ben stopped and held her hand a moment. "No chocolate, Susie," he said gently.

Like a child, her eyes filled with tears. Ben stooped to give her grimy wrinkled cheek a kiss, then rushed up the stairs and out into the open air.

No hesitation as he turned into Morrison Street. He knew exactly where he was going. To Greenbriars. To Caroline.

To the one person on the face of the earth who cared about him. To the only person who treated him as a human being and not some half-wild animal who smelled of dirty clothes and rotting food.

Ben hadn't eaten in two days, and he had only a too-short cotton jacket on to keep the cold away. His big, bony wrists stuck out of the jacket's sleeves, and he had to tuck his hands into his armpits to keep them warm.

No matter. He'd been cold and hungry before.

The only warm thing he wanted right now was Caroline's smile.

Like the arrow of a compass to a lodestar, he leaned into the wind to walk the mile and a half to Greenbriars.

No one looked his way as he trudged by. He was invisible, a lone, tall figure dressed in rags. It didn't bother him. He'd always been invisible. Being invisible had helped him survive.

The weather worsened. The wind blew icy needles of sleet directly into his eyes until he had to close them into slits.

Didn't matter. He had an excellent sense of direction and could make his way to Greenbriars blindfolded.

Head down, arms wrapped around himself to conserve what little warmth he'd been able to absorb at the shelter, Ben slowly left behind the dark, sullen buildings of the part of the city that housed the shelter. Soon the roads opened up into tree-lined avenues. Ancient brick buildings gave way to graceful, modern buildings of glass and steel.

No cars passed—the weather was too severe for that. There was nobody on the streets. Under his feet, the icy buildup crackled.

He was almost there. The houses were big here, in this wealthy part of town. Large, well built, with sloping green lawns that were now covered in ice and snow.

He usually made his way through the back streets, invisible as always. Someone like him in this place of rich and powerful people would be immediately stopped by the police, so he always took the back streets on a normal day. But today the streets were deserted, and he walked openly on the broad sidewalks.

It usually took him half an hour to walk to Greenbriars but today the ice-slick sidewalks and hard wind dragged at him. An hour after leaving the shelter, he was still walking. He was strong, but hunger and cold started to wear him down. His feet, in their cracked shoes, were numb.

Music sounded, so lightly at first that he wondered whether he was hallucinating from cold and hunger. Notes floated in the air, as if borne by the snow.

He rounded a corner and there it was—Greenbriars. Caroline's home. His heart pounded as it loomed out of the sleety mist.

It always pounded when he came here, just as it pounded whenever she was near.

He usually came in through the back entrance, when her parents were at work and Caroline and her brother in school. The maid left at noon and from noon to one the house was his to explore. He could move in and out like a ghost. The back door lock was flimsy, and he'd been picking locks since he was five.

He'd wander from room to room, soaking up the rich, scented atmosphere of Caroline's home.

The shelter rarely had hot water, but still he took care to wash as well as he could whenever he headed out to Greenbriars. The stench of the shelter had no place in Caroline's home.

Greenbriars was so far beyond what he could ever hope to have that there was no jealousy, no envy in him as he touched the backs of the thousands of books in the library, walked into sweet-smelling closets full of new clothes, opened the huge refrigerator to see fresh fruits and vegetables. Caroline's family was rich in a way he couldn't comprehend, as if they belonged to a different species living on another planet.

To him, it was simply Caroline's world. And living in it for an hour a day was like touching the sky.

Today nobody could see him approach in the storm. He walked right up the driveway, feeling the gravel through the thin soles of his shoes. The snow intensified, the wind whipping painful icy particles through the air. Ben knew how to move quietly, stealthily when he had to. But it wasn't necessary now. There was no one to see him or hear him as he crunched his way to the window.

The music was louder now, the source a yellow glow. It wasn't until he had reached the end of the driveway that Ben realized that the yellow glow was the big twelve-pane window of the living room, and the music was someone playing the piano.

He knew that living room well, as he knew all the rooms of the big mansion. He'd wandered them all, for hours. He knew that the huge living room always smelled faintly of woodsmoke from the big fireplace. He knew that the couches were deep and comfortable and the rugs soft and thick.

He walked straight up to the window. The snow was already filling in the tracks his shoes made. No one could see him, no one could hear him.

He was tall, and could see over the windowsill if he stood on tiptoe. Light had drained from the sky, and he knew no one in the room could see him outside.

The living room was like something out of a painting. Hundreds of candles flickered everywhere—on the mantelpiece, on all the tables. The coffee table held the remains of a feast—half a ham on a carving board, a huge loaf of bread, a big platter of cheeses, several cakes, and two pies. A teapot, cups, glasses, an open bottle of wine, a bottle of whiskey.

Water pooled in his mouth. He hadn't eaten for two days. His empty stomach ached. He could almost smell the food in the room through the windowpane.

Then food completely disappeared from his mind.

A lovely voice rang out, clear and pure, singing a Christmas carol he'd heard in a shopping mall once while he helped his dad panhandle. Something about a shepherd boy.

It was Caroline's voice. He'd recognize it anywhere.

A frigid gust of wind buffeted the garden, raking his face with sleet. He didn't even feel it as he edged his head farther up over the windowsill.

There she was! As always, his breath caught when he saw her.

She was so beautiful, it sometimes hurt him to look at her. When she visited him in the shelter, he'd refuse to look at her for the first few minutes. It was like looking into the sun.

He watched her hungrily, committing each second to memory. He remembered every word she'd ever spoken to him, he'd read and reread every book she'd ever brought him, he remembered every item of clothing he'd ever seen her in.

She was at the piano, playing. He'd never seen anyone actually play the piano, and it seemed like magic to him. Her fingers moved gracefully over the black and white keys, and music poured out like water in a stream. His head filled with the wonder of it.

She was in profile. Her eyes were closed as she played, a slight smile on her face, as if she and the music shared a secret understanding. She was singing another song even he recognized. "Silent Night." Her voice rose, pure and light.

The piano was tall and black, with lit candles held in shiny brass holders along the sides.

Though the entire room was filled with candles, Caroline glowed more brightly than any of them. She was lit with light, her pale skin gleaming in the glowing candlelight as she sang and played.

The song came to an end, and her hands dropped to her lap. She looked up, smiling, at the applause, then started another carol, her voice rising pure and high.

The whole family was there. Mr. Lake, a big-shot businessman, tall, blond, looking like the king of the world. Mrs. Lake, *impossibly beautiful and elegant. Toby, Caroline's seven-year-old brother. There was another person in the room, a handsome young man. He was elegantly dressed, his dark blond hair combed straight back. His fingers were beating time with the carol on the piano top. When Caroline stopped playing, he leaned down and gave her a kiss on the mouth.*

Caroline's parents laughed, and Toby did a somersault on the big rug.

Caroline smiled up at the handsome young man and said something that made him laugh. He bent to kiss her hair.

Ben watched, his heart nearly stopping.

This was Caroline's boyfriend. Of course. They shared a look—blond, poised, privileged. Good-looking, rich, educated. They belonged to the same species. They were meant to be together, it was so clear.

His heart slowed in his chest. For the first time, he felt the danger from the cold. He felt its icy fingers reaching out to him to drag him down to where his father had gone.

Maybe he should just let it take him.

There was nothing for him here, in this lovely candlelit room. He would never be a part of this world. He belonged to the darkness and the cold.

Ben dropped back down on his heels, backing slowly away from the house until the yellow light of the window was lost in the sleet and mist. He was shaking with the cold as he trudged back down the driveway, the wet snow seeping through the holes in his shoes to soak his feet.

Half an hour later, he came to the interstate junction and stopped, swaying on his feet.

The human in him wanted to sink to the ground, curl up in a ball, and wait for despair and then death to take him, as they had taken his father. It wouldn't take long.

But the animal in him was strong and wanted, fiercely, to live.

To the right, the road stretched northward, right up into Canada. To the left, it went south.

If he went north, he would die. It was as simple as that.

Turning left, Ben shuffled forward, head low, into the icy wind.

Dangerous Secrets

CHAPTER ONE

Parker's Ridge

"Read any good books lately?"

The pretty young woman stacking books and sorting papers in the Parker's Ridge County Library turned around in surprise. It was closing time and the library wasn't overwhelmed with people at the best of times. By closing time it was always deserted. Nick Ireland should know. He'd been staking it out for a week.

"Oh! Hello, Mr. Ames." Her cheeks pinked with pleasure at seeing him. "Did you need something else?" She checked the big old-fashioned clock on the wall. "We're closing up, but I can stay on for another quarter of an hour if you need anything."

He'd been in that morning and she'd been charmingly

helpful to him. Or, rather, to Nicholas Ames, stockbroker, retired from the Wall Street rat race after several years of very lucky investments paid off big, now looking to start his own investment firm. Son of Keith and Amanda Ames, investment banker and family lawyer, respectively, both tragically dead at a young age. Nicholas Ames was thirty-four years old, a Capricorn, divorced after a short-lived starter marriage in his twenties, collector of vintage wines, affable, harmless, all-round good guy.

Not a word of that was true. Not one word.

They were alone in the library, which pleased him and annoyed him at the same time. It pleased him because he'd have Charity Prewitt's undivided attention. It annoyed him because . . . because.

Because through the huge library windows she looked like a lovely little lamb staked out for the predators. It had been dark for an hour up here in this frozen northern state. In the well-lit library, Charity Prewitt had been showcased against the darkness of the evening. One very pretty young woman all alone in an enclosed space. It screamed out to any passing scumbag—*come and get me!*

Nothing scumbags liked better than to eat up lovely young women. If there was one thing Nick knew with every fiber of his being, it was that the world was full of scumbags. He'd been fighting them all his life.

She was smiling up at him, much, *much* prettier than the photographs in the file he'd studied.

"No, thank you, Miss Prewitt," he answered, keeping his deep, naturally rough voice gentle. "I don't need to do any more research. You were very helpful this morning."

Her head tilted, the soft dark-blond hair brushing her right shoulder. "Did you have a good day, then?"

"Yes, I did, a very good day. Thank you for asking. I saw three factories, a promising new Web design start-up, and an old-economy sawmill that has some very innovative ideas about using recycled wood chips. All in all, very satisfactory."

Actually, it had been a shitty day, just one of many shitty days on this mission. A total waste of time spent in the surveillance van with two smelly men and jack shit to show for it except for one cryptic call to Worontzoff about a friend staying safe.

Nick smiled the satisfaction he didn't feel. "So. It's closing time now, isn't it?"

She smiled back. "Why, yes. We close at six. But as I said, if you need something—"

"Well, to tell you the truth . . ." Nick looked down at his shoes shyly, as if working up the courage to ask. Man, he loved looking down at those shoes. They were three-hundred-dollar Italian imports, worlds away from his usual comfortable but battered combat boots that dated back to his army days.

Being Nicholas Ames, very successful businessman, was great because he got to dress the part and Uncle Sam had to foot the bill. He had an entire wardrobe to fit those magnificent shoes. Who knew if he'd get to keep any of it? Maybe the two Armanis that had been specially tailored for his broad shoulders.

And even better was dealing with this librarian, Charity Prewitt, one of the prettiest women he'd ever seen. Small, curvy, classy with large eyes the color of the sea at dawn.

Nick looked up from contemplating his black shiny wingtips and smiled into her beautiful gray eyes. "Actually, I was hoping that I could invite you out to dinner to thank you for your help. If I hadn't done this preliminary research here, with your able help, my day wouldn't have been half as productive. Asking you out to dinner is the least I can do to show you my appreciation."

She blinked. "Well . . . ," she began.

"You have nothing to fear from me," he said hastily. "I'm a solid citizen—just ask my accountant and my physician. And I'm perfectly harmless."

He wasn't, of course, he was dangerous as hell. Ten years a Delta operator before joining the Unit. He'd spent the past decade in black ops, perfecting the art of killing people.

He was sure harmless to *her*, though.

Charity Prewitt had the most delicious skin he'd ever seen on a woman—pale ivory with a touch of rose underneath—so delicate it looked like it would bruise if he so much as breathed on it. That was skin meant for touching and stroking, not hurting.

"Ms. Prewitt?" She hadn't answered his question about going out. She simply stood there, head tilted to one side, watching him as if he were some kind of problem to be sorted out, but she needed more information before she could solve it.

In a way, he liked that. She didn't jump at the invitation, which was a welcome relief from his last date—well, last fuck. Five minutes after "hello" in a bar, she'd had his dick in her hand. At least she hadn't been into pain like Consuelo. God.

Charity Prewitt was assessing him quietly and he let her do it, understanding that smooth words weren't going to do the trick. Stillness would, so he stood still. Special Forces soldiers have the gift of stillness. The ones who don't, die young and badly.

Nick was engaging in a little assessment himself. This morning he'd been bowled over by little Miss Charity Prewitt. Christ, with a name like that, with her job as chief librarian of the library of a one-traffic-light town, single at twenty-eight, he'd been expecting a dried-up prune.

The photographs of her in his file had been fuzzy, taken with a telescopic lens, and just showed the generics—hair and skin color, general size and shape. A perfectly normal woman. A little on the small side, but other than that, ordinary.

But up close and personal, Jesus, she'd turned out to be a knockout. A quiet knockout. You had to look twice for the full impact of large light-gray eyes, porcelain skin, shiny dark-blond hair and a curvy slender figure to make itself felt. Coupled with a natural elegance and a soft, attractive voice—well.

Nick was used to being undercover, but most of his jobs involved scumbags, not beautiful young women.

Actually, this one did, too—a major scumbag called Vassily Worontzoff everyone on earth but the operatives in the Unit revered for being a great writer. Even nominated for the friggin' Nobel, though, as the Unit knew well but couldn't yet prove, the sick fuck was the head of a huge international OC syndicate. Nick was intent on bringing him down.

So on this op he was dealing with scumbags, yeah, but the mission also involved romancing this pretty woman—and on Uncle Sam's dime, to boot.

Didn't get much better than that.

"All right," Charity said suddenly. Whatever her doubts had been, apparently they were now cleared up. "What time do you want to pick me up?"

Yes! Nick felt a surge of energy that had nothing to do with the mission and everything to do with the woman in front of him.

"Well . . ." Nick smiled, all affable, utterly safe, utterly reliable businessman, "I was wondering whether you wouldn't mind going now. I found this fabulous Italian place near Rockville. It has a really nice bar area and I thought we might talk over a drink while waiting for our dinner."

"Da Emilio's," Charity said. "It's a very nice place and the food is excellent." She looked down at herself, frowning. "But I'm not dressed for a dinner out. I should go home and change."

She was wearing a light blue-gray sweater that exactly matched the color of her eyes and hugged round breasts and a narrow waist, a slim black skirt, shiny black stockings, and pretty ankle boots. Pearl necklace and pearl earrings. She was the classiest-looking dame he'd seen in a long while, even in her work clothes.

"You look—" *Perfect. Sexy as hell.* He bit his jaws closed on the words. Ireland, roughneck soldier that he was, could say something like that, but Ames, sophisticated businessman, sure as hell couldn't. Even if it was God's own truth. "Fine. You look just fine. You could go to dinner at the White House dressed like that."

It made her smile, which was what he wanted. Her smile

was like a secret weapon. She sighed. "Okay. I'll just need to lock up here."

Locking up entailed pulling the library door closed and turning a key once in the lock.

Nick waited. Charity looked up at him, a tiny frown between her brows when she saw his scowl. "Is something wrong?"

"That's it? That's locking up? Turning the key once in the lock?"

She smiled gently. "This isn't the big bad city, Mr. Ames."

"My friends call me Nick."

"Okay, Nick. I don't know if you've had a chance to walk around town. This isn't New York or even Burlington. The library, in case you haven't noticed, is full of books and not much else besides some scuffed tables. What would there be to steal? And anyway, I don't remember the last time a crime was committed in Parker's Ridge."

The elation Nick felt at the thought of an evening with Charity Prewitt dissipated.

Parker's Ridge housed one of the world's most dangerous criminals. An evil man. A man directly responsible for hundreds of lives lost, for untold misery and suffering.

And he was Charity Prewitt's best friend.

Dangerous Passion

CHAPTER ONE

Alleyway outside the Feinstein Art Gallery
Manhattan
November 17

Feelings kill faster than bullets, that old Russian army saying, raced through Viktor "Drake" Drakovich's mind when he heard the noise behind him. It was barely audible. The faint sound of metal against leather, fabric against fabric and the softest whisper of a metallic click.

The sound of a gun being pulled from its holster, the safety being switched off. He'd heard a variation of this sound thousands and thousands of times over the years.

He'd known for a year now that this moment would come. It was only a question of when, not if. He'd been barreling toward it, against every instinct in his body, completely out of control, for a full year.

From his boyhood living wild on the streets of Odessa, he'd survived the most brutal conditions possible, over and over again, by being cautious, by never exposing himself unnecessarily, by being security conscious, always.

What he'd been doing for the past year was the equivalent of suicide.

It didn't feel that way, though.

It felt like . . . like life itself.

He could remember to the second when his life changed. Utterly, completely, instantly.

He'd been in his limousine, separated from Mischa, his driver, by the soundproof partition. In the car he never talked, and used the time to catch up on paperwork. It had been years since he'd driven anywhere for pleasure. Cars were to get from A to B, when he couldn't fly.

The windows were heavily smoked. For security, of course. But also because it had been a long time since the outside world had interested him enough to glance out the windows at the passing scenery.

The heavy armor-plated Mercedes S600 was stopped in traffic. The overhead stoplight continued cycling through the colors, green-yellow-red, green-yellow-red, over and over again, but traffic was at a standstill. Something had happened up ahead. The blare of impatient horns filtered through the armored walls and bulletproof glass of his car, sounding as if coming from far away, like the buzzing of crazed insects in the distance.

A motorcycle eased past the cars like an eel in water. One

driver was so enraged at the sight of the motorcyclist making headway, he leaned angrily on his horn, rolled down the window and stuck his middle finger up in the air. He shouted something out, red faced, spittle flying.

Drake closed his eyes in disgust. Even in America, where there was order and plenty and peace—even here there was aggression and envy. Humans never learned. They were like violent children, petulant and greedy and out of control.

It was an old feeling, dating from his childhood, as familiar to him as the feel of his hands and feet. Humans were flawed and rapacious and violent. You used that, profited from it and stayed as much out of their way as possible. It was the closest thing to a creed he had and it had served him well all his life.

Oddly enough, though, lately this kind of thinking had made him . . . impatient. Annoyed. Wanting to step away from it all. Go . . . somewhere else. Do something else. *Be* someone else.

If there were another world, he'd emigrate to it. But there was only this world, filled with greedy and violent people.

Whenever he found himself in this mood, which was more and more often lately, he tried to shake himself out of it. Moods were an excellent way to get killed.

Strangely out of sorts, he looked again at the spreadsheets on his lap. They tracked a 10-million-dollar contract to supply weapons to a Tajikistani warlord, the first of what Drake hoped would be several deals with the self-styled "general." There was newfound oil in the general's fiefdom, a goddamned lake of it right underneath the barren, hard-packed earth, and the general was in the mood to buy whatever was necessary to hold on to the power and the oil. When this deal went through smoothly, as it certainly would, Drake knew there would be many more down the line.

Years ago, if nothing else, the thought would have given him satisfaction. Now, he felt nothing at all. It was a business deal. He would put in the work; it would net him more money. Nothing he hadn't done thousands and thousands of times before.

He stared at the printouts until they blurred, trying to drum up interest in the deal. It wasn't there, which was alarming. What was even more alarming was the dull void in his chest as he reflected on his indifference. Not being able to care about not being able to care was frightening. Would have been frightening, if he could work up the energy to be frightened.

Restless, he glanced to his right. This section of Lexington was full of bookshops and art galleries, the shop windows more pleasing, less crass than the boutiques with their stupid, outlandish clothes a block uptown.

And that was when he saw them.

Paintings. A wall of them, together with a few watercolors and ink drawings. All heartbreakingly beautiful, all clearly by the same fine hand. A hand even he recognized was extraordinary.

Though the car windows were smoked, the gallery was well lit and each work of art had its own wall-mounted spotlight, so Drake got a good look at them all, stalled there in a mid-Manhattan traffic jam. And anyway, his eyesight was sniper grade.

He did something he'd never done before. He buzzed

down his window. The driver's mouth fell open. Drake flicked his gaze to the rearview mirror. The driver's mouth snapped shut and his face assumed an impassive expression.

The car instantly filled with the smell of exhaust fumes and the loud cacophony of a Manhattan traffic jam.

Drake ignored it completely. The important thing was he had a better view of the paintings now.

The first painting he saw took his breath away. A simple image—a woman alone at sunset on a long, empty beach. The rendering of the sea, the colors of the sunset, the grainy beach—all those details were technically perfect. But what came off the surface of the painting like steam off an iron was the loneliness of the woman. It could have been the portrait of the last human on earth.

The Mercedes lurched forward a foot then stopped. He barely noticed.

The paintings were like little miracles on a wall. A glowing still life of wildflowers in a can and an open paperback on a table, as if someone had just come in from the garden. A pensive man reflecting himself in a shop window. Delicate female hands holding a book. The artwork was realistic, delicate, stunning. It pulled you in to the world of the picture and didn't let you go.

Drake had no way to judge the artwork in technical terms; all he knew was that each work was brilliant, perfect, and called to him in some way he'd never felt before.

The car rolled forward ten feet, bringing another section of the wall into view.

The last painting on the wall jolted him.

It was the left profile of a man rendered in earth tones.

The man's face was hard, strong-jawed, unsmiling. His dark hair was cut so short the skull beneath was visible, which was exactly as Drake wore it in the field, particularly in Afghanistan. Far from even the faintest hope of running water, he shaved his head and his body hair, the only way to avoid lice. The face of the man didn't exactly look like him, but the portrait had the look of him—features harsh, grim, unyielding.

Running from the forehead over the high cheekbone and down to the jaw, brushing perilously close to the left eye, was a ragged white scar, like a lightning bolt etched in flesh.

Reflexively, Drake lifted a hand to his face, remembering.

He'd been a street rat on the streets of Odessa, sleeping in a doorway in the dead of winter. Some warmth seeped through the cracks in the door, allowing him to sleep without fear of freezing to death in the subzero temperatures.

Emaciated, dressed in rags, he was perfect prey for the sailors just ashore from months working brutal shifts at sea, reeling drunk through the streets. Sailors who hadn't had sex in months and didn't much care who they fucked—boy or girl—as long as whoever it was held still long enough. Most of the sailors didn't even care whether who they fucked stayed still because they were tied down or dead.

Drake came awake in a rush as the fetid breath of two Russian sailors washed over his face. One of the sailors held a knife to Drake's throat while the other dropped his pants, already hauling out a long, thin, beet-red cock.

Drake was a born street fighter and fought best when he was close to the ground. He was born with the ability and had honed it by observation and practice. He scissored his legs, bringing the man with the knife toppling to the ground, then hurled himself at the knees of the second man, hobbled by his pants. The man fell heavily to the ground, his head hitting the broken pavement with a sickening crack.

Drake turned to the first man, who'd scrambled to his feet and was holding the knife in front of him like an expert, edge down. The chances of surviving a knife fight barehanded were ludicrously low. Drake knew he had to even the odds fast, do something unexpected.

He flung himself forward, into the knife. The blade sliced the side of his face open, but the surprise move loosened the sailor's grip. Drake wrenched the knife out of his hand and jabbed it into the man's eye, to the hilt.

The sailor dropped like a stone.

Drake stood over him, panting, his blood dripping over the man's face, then pulled the knife out of his attacker's skull and wiped it down on the man's tattered jacket.

He took both men's knives. One was a *nozh razvedchika*, a scout's knife. The other was a Finnish Pukka, rare in those parts and very valuable. He bartered both along the Odessa waterfront for two guns, a Skorpion and an AK–47—including clips and shooting lessons—sold cheaply because they were stolen.

He was on his way.

Later, as soon as he could afford it, he had plastic surgery on the long, jagged white scar on the left side of his face. He was known for being able to blend into almost any environment, for turning himself invisible, but a very visible scar was like a flag, something no one forgot. It had to go.

The surgeon was good, one of the best. There was nothing

visible left of his scar. Besides himself, only the surgeon could remember the shape of the long-gone scar. But there it was, in a painting in a gallery in Manhattan, half a world away and two decades later. However crazy it sounded, the scar in the painting was the same scar the surgeon had eliminated, all those years ago.

Traffic suddenly cleared and the Mercedes rolled smoothly forward. Drake punched the button in the center console that allowed him to communicate with the driver.

"Sir?" Mischa sounded startled over the intercom. Drake rarely spoke while they were traveling.

"Turn right at the next intersection and let me off after two blocks."

"*Sir?*" This time the driver's voice sounded confused. Drake never left the car en route. He got into one of his many vehicles in his building's garage and got out at his destination. The driver caught himself. Drake never had to repeat himself with his men. "Yessir," the driver replied.

Once out of the limousine, Drake continued walking in the direction of the car until it disappeared into the traffic, then ducked into a nearby department store. Ten minutes later, satisfied that he wasn't being followed, he doubled back to the art gallery, having ditched his eight-hundred-dollar Boss jacket, Brioni pants, Armani cashmere sweater and scarf and having bought a cheap parka, long-sleeved cotton tee, jeans, watch cap and sunglasses. He was as certain as he could be that no one was tailing him and that he was unrecognizable.

The art gallery was warm after the chill of the street. Drake stopped just inside the door, taking in the scent of tea brewing and that mixture of expensive perfumes and men's cologne typical of Manhattan haunts, mixed with the more down-to-earth smells of resin and solvents.

At the sound of the bell over the door, a man came out from a back room, smiling, holding a porcelain mug. Steam rose in white fingers from the mug.

"Hello and welcome." The man transferred the mug from his right hand to his left and offered his hand. "My name is Harold Feinstein. Welcome to the Feinstein Gallery."

The smile seemed genuine, not a salesman's smile. Drake had seen too many of those from people who knew who he was and knew what resources he could command. Everything that could possibly be sold—including humans—had been offered to him, with a smile.

But the man holding his hand out couldn't know who he was, and wasn't presuming he was rich. Not dressed the way he was.

Drake took the proffered hand gingerly, not remembering the last time he'd clasped another man's hand. He touched other people rarely, not even during sex. Usually, he employed his hands to keep his torso up and away from the woman.

Harold Feinstein's hand was soft, well-manicured, but the grip was surprisingly strong.

"Have a look around," he urged. "No need to buy. Art enriches us all, whether we own it or not."

Without seeming to study him, Feinstein had taken in the cheap clothes and pegged him as a window-shopper, but wasn't bothered by it. Unusual in a man of commerce.

Drake's eyes traversed the wall and Harold Feinstein turned amiably.

"Take my latest discovery," he said, waving his free hand. "Grace Larsen. Remarkable eye for detail, amazing technical expertise, perfect brush strokes. Command of chiaroscuro in the etchings. Quite remarkable."

The artist was a *woman*? Drake focused on the paintings. Man, woman, whoever the artist was, the work was extraordinary. And now that he was here, he could see that a side wall, invisible from the street, was covered with etchings and watercolors.

He stopped in front of an oil, a portrait of an old woman. She was stooped, graying, hair pulled back in a bun, face weatherbeaten from the sun, large hands gnarled from physical labor, dressed in a cheap cotton print dress. She looked as if she were just about to step down from the painting, drop to her knees and start scrubbing the floor.

Yet she was beautiful, because the artist saw her as beautiful. A specific woman, the very epitome of a female workhorse, the kind that held the world together with her labor. Drake had seen that woman in the thousands, toiling in fields around the world, sweeping the streets of Moscow.

All the sorrow and strength of the human race was right there, in her sloping shoulders and tired eyes.

Amazing.

The door behind him chimed as someone entered the gallery.

Feinstein straightened, his smile broadened. "And here's the artist herself." He looked at Drake, dressed in his poor clothes. "Take your time and enjoy the paintings," he said gently.

Drake smelled her before he saw her. A fresh smell, like

spring and sunshine, not a perfume. Completely out of place in the fumes of midtown Manhattan. His first thought was, *No woman can live up to that smell.*

"Hello, Harold," he heard a woman's voice say behind him. "I brought some india-ink drawings. I thought you might like to look at them. And I finished the waterfront. Stayed up all night to do it." The voice was soft, utterly female, with a smile in it.

His second thought was, *No woman can live up to that voice.* The voice was soft, melodic, seeming to hit him like a note on a tuning fork, reverberating through him so strongly he actually had to concentrate on the words.

Drake turned—and stared.

His entire body froze. He found himself completely incapable of moving for a heartbeat—two—until he managed to shake himself from his paralysis by sheer force of will.

Something—some atavistic survival instinct dwelling deep in his DNA—made him turn away so she wouldn't see him full face, but he had excellent peripheral vision and he watched intently as the woman—Grace—opened a big portfolio carrier and started laying out heavy sheets of paper, setting them out precisely on a huge glass table. Then she brought out what looked like a spool of 10-inch-wide paper from her purse.

Goddamn. The woman was . . . exquisite.

Be Impulsive!

Look for Other
Avon Impulse Authors

www.AvonImpulse.com